MURDER AT THE MINE

A ROSE BLAIR MURDER MYSTERY

JUDY KEIGHTLEY

COZY HOUSE PRESS

COZY HOUSE PRESS
MAKE A DATE WITH MURDER

An Imprint for GracePoint Publishing (www.GracePointPublishing.com)

GracePoint Matrix, LLC
624 S. Cascade Ave
Suite 201
Colorado Springs, CO 80903
www.GracePointMatrix.com
Email: Admin@GracePointMatrix.com
SAN # 991-6032

ISBN-13: (Paperback) –978-1-951694-56-2
eISBN: (eBook) - 978-1-951694-55-5

MAKE A DATE WITH MURDER...

Find Cozy House Press online to read more great cozy mysteries!

www.cozyhousepress.com

COZY HOUSE PRESS
MAKE A DATE WITH MURDER

FOREWORD

I carry all my novels around with me like an old bag filling it with ideas and thoughts like a magpie as I go along. During a period of six months, I begin to put my collection of ideas together to form the basis of my story until I'm ready to start researching and making copious notes.

This year, however proved to a very challenging one for everyone. Gone were my friends whom I would normally brainstorm ideas and share a good laugh. The COVID-19 virus put an end to interacting not only with friends but with the library where normally I would spend hours sourcing out information. Isolation can be a writer's best friend, but it can also be her enemy.

I became quite indecisive, and my biggest problem lay in whether to mention the pandemic in my book or not. The trouble was if I started to talk about the lockdowns and the isolation where would I stop and I certainly did not want *Mining for Murder* to become a depressing read.

Therefore, I deliberately omitted any mention of the

horrible year that not only myself, but the whole world has experienced, and so I apologize to all my readers as I normally do try to keep the content of my Rose Blair Murder Mysteries on topic and up to date with current affairs.

As usual I give a huge thank you to my darling, ever patient husband, for supporting me through this stressful period, particularly over the past month, when writing this novel became all consuming. To my editing readers, Alison, Paulette, and Kate, I am forever indebted to you.

I hope that you, the reader, enjoy this, my ninth Rose Blair Murder mystery.

ONE

Roy looked at least ten years younger in death, Tom thought wryly as he slowly walked past the open casket at the funeral home in Zurich. He glanced over to the long line-up of friends and family come to say their final farewell to a man well loved in the community. Tom, himself, hadn't known Roy that long, but in the short time that he had Tom had enjoyed the company of the man who became one of his golfing buddies and fellow "Thirsty-Thursday" acquaintance. Indeed, there were at least eight of the guys who participated in the Thursday afternoon social gathering held at the Black Dog, and hence the name, who were attending Roy's visitation.

Tom caught the eye of George who was about to shake the hand of Roy's wife Eileen in the line-up. George, Roy, and Tom had recently got to know each other quite well and had formed a close friendship. In fact, the day that Roy had died the three men had planned to play golf together and then Roy had fallen down the stairs at the end of Pavilion Road when taking his dog, Pee-Wee, for a walk. He had broken his neck and died instantly. Pee-Wee, his Jack Russell terrier, had run home, his leash still attached to his collar and had howled outside Roy and Eileen's front door until Eileen heard the commotion and went to find her husband. It barely seemed possible, Tom thought, that he would never play golf or drink a pint with his friend Roy ever again. Lost in his sad thoughts Tom never heard Alex come up to him. It was only when he patted Tom on his shoulder that he looked up.

"Oh, Alex, sorry, I was deep in thought. Rum affair, isn't it?"

Alex looked sombre, "Sure is, Tom, sure is. You never know when your cards are up, do you? How old was Roy?"

Tom hadn't known the answer to that question until just ten minutes ago when he had read the obituary posted by the funeral home. Roy had been born in 1949, making him just seventy-two. He was far too young to die.

Rose walked over to Tom and, looking at Alex, she held out her hand in greeting saying, "Hi, I'm Rose, Tom's wife. I don't think that we've met before."

Tom cleared his throat, "Sorry, love, this is Alex, he's a relatively new member of our Thirsty Thursday's group."

Alex smiled as he shook Rose's hand. "Yes, I've only been in the village a few months and already feel as if I belong. It's such a friendly community."

"Have you retired here, Alex, or are you still working?"

Rose never got an answer as George ambled over and interrupted their conversation.

"Alex, Tom, I'd like to have a quick word with you if you don't mind. Oh, I'm sorry, Rose, but it is important."

The three men walked to the other side of the room away

from the crowds. Rose glanced at them, but was soon distracted by Jean, George's wife, who had stopped to chat.

"Just what are those men talking about? Have you noticed anything different about Tom, Rose?" Jean asked seriously.

Rose didn't know George's wife very well but she played Mah-jong every Monday at the library and Rose had chatted to her there on and off. Jean seemed to be a pleasant woman, friendly and warm.

"Well, now that you mention it, Tom hasn't been quite himself lately. He's been very preoccupied and self-absorbed."

"Yes, George has been too. I wonder what exactly is going on."

It would be a while before Rose received any answers to Tom's preoccupation. Indeed, as the next tragedy unfolded she wondered if that conversation with Jean was in one way or another a premonition, a foreshadowing of the impending macabre events about to unfold.

On Sunday, June 4th, George went for his usual cycle ride down Orchard Line. It was a beautiful summer's morning with not a single cloud in the sky, just a slight breeze in the air: perfect weather for cycling. Just passed The Berry Farm, with no warning, a large SUV appeared from seemingly nowhere. It accelerated fast and ploughed deliberately into the back of George on his bicycle killing him instantly. There were no witnesses. George died four hours later from massive internal haemorrhaging. The driver of the vehicle was never found, and his death was recorded as an accident. His funeral took place exactly one week after Roy's, giving Rose and Tom much pause for thought.

Tom felt extremely agitated and very nervous. The fact that he had lost two of his closest mates in less than a week, had left him feeling profoundly sad and confused. His last conversation with George and Alex, ironically at their friend Roy's funeral, kept echoing in his thoughts like a stuck record. George, usually a mild-mannered man, had been quite angry with Alex and his last words to Tom were that he wanted to speak to him in private.

Just that morning Jean had phoned Tom to let him know that George had left an envelope addressed to Tom. He had popped in his car and picked up the letter with some trepidation. On some subconscious level Tom already knew what the contents would be, so it came as no surprise when Tom found a copy of George's shareholders certificate with Section 12 highlighted in yellow. Tom read the small print three times over before letting out a deep heart felt sigh. Under his breath he muttered, "Oh, bugger, bugger, bugger."

Three months ago, George, Roy, Alex, and Tom were in a celebratory mood. All four of them had formed a small consortium of shareholders to invest in a silver mine up north, near Timmins, Ontario. They had all put in equal amounts of money - $200,000 each to be exact. Alex had been the instigator of the consortium, telling the men that their money would be tripled by years end.

None of them had told their wives, indeed they had made a pact that they would not mention the investment to anyone else; it would be their private investment and ultimate profit. Not telling Rose that he had invested a significant portion of their retirement savings had not sat well with Tom. He wasn't one for keeping secrets and it had weighed heavily on him for weeks now that the initial euphoria had worn off.

It had crossed his mind fleetingly as to what would happen to the consortium now that two out of the four investors were no longer around; what would actually happen to the shares? This question was answered by the letter attached to the shareholders certificate marked up by George. According to Section 12, if any shareholder should pass away the other shareholders would automatically inherit their shares so that now Alex and Tom were both fifty percent shareholders of the Silvercorp consortium. In George's letter he had argued that they needed to look into the mine and find out more about Alex. Alarm bells had obviously been ringing in George's ears and Tom began to hear them too. If two of his friends had died, supposedly from accidental deaths, would not his demise make Alex the sole beneficiary of the consortium? This thought kept playing through Tom's mind again and again. Would he be the next to die?

TWO

Rose took another batch of scones out from the oven. It was the Croquet Club's Women's Social that afternoon and she had promised to bake two dozen for the event. Rose had already made a dozen orange and cranberry scones and was about to make a batch of blueberry scones, when the telephone rang. It was Jessica from Montreal.

"Hi, Mom. I just wanted to check that it's still okay for Abby and Ella to stay for the first week in July? I'm in the middle of booking various summer camps for them and I've kept that first week of their summer holidays free. Would the first week in July or the second week in August still work for Dad and you?"

Rose glanced at her calendar. She had reverted to using a large calendar which now hung from a hook on her pantry door. Before, she used a hand-held planner, but this old-fashioned way was much better as she could glance at it when she was cooking or on the phone like she was doing right now and could see that both weeks Jessica had mentioned were free.

"Yes, that will be fine, darling. We look forward to seeing the girls again. Will you and Rob be staying for the weekend when you drop them off?"

There was a long pause on the line and then Jessica said, "Well, here's the thing, Mom, we wondered if you and Dad could maybe meet us halfway- we thought maybe Kingston? It would shorten the journey substantially for us."

Rose thought about it. Kingston was a good five hours away from Bayfield. That would mean five hours there and five hours back, ten hours of travelling time all in one day. Tom would certainly not want to do that, but they could, of course, book an Airbnb for the night and make a little holiday out of it, maybe visit the Thousand Islands and Gananoque.

"Let me think about that, dear. I'll have to talk to your father as it's an awfully long way to travel there and back in one day. I'll get back to you soon. Okay?"

Thinking of Airbnb's made Rose glance at the calendar again. Her sister Kate's cottage had been solidly booked on Airbnb all throughout the month of June and through to August. Since Kate had moved to London, Rose and Tom had offered to look after her cottage, meet and greet the guests, and generally clean up after they had departed.

Today a new batch of guests would be checking-in and she would have to go over to leave some milk and a bottle of wine in the fridge and put some fresh-cut flowers in a vase on the table. Clean sheets and towels were already stacked neatly on the beds in the cottage and the place had already been thoroughly cleaned. Rose called to Tom who was busy in the study.

"Tom, do you want to come with me to get Kate's place ready for the next guests? Oh, and by the way, you'll have to meet them as I'm playing croquet this afternoon, it's the Women's Social."

There was no response from the study, so Rose walked over and opened the door to find Tom on the computer, deep in thought. On the screen there looked to be a picture of a mine and the word, "Silvercorp" scrolled across.

"Tom, did you hear anything that I said?"

He turned his head slowly to look at Rose blankly and then he shook his head.

"Sorry love, I was a million miles away. Could you repeat what you just said?"

This will have to stop, Rose thought as she repeated herself concluding with, "Tom, what on earth is wrong with you? You seem so preoccupied. Tell me, what's the problem?"

Tom looked glumly at the screen and then back at Rose.

"Sit down love and I'll tell you what a silly bugger I've been and how scared I am now for the consequences of my actions."

Rose looked alarmed, but for once said nothing as she pulled another chair over and sat down quietly waiting for Tom to begin.

Tom began to talk softly, outlining how Alex had joined the Thirsty Thursday's men's social group and how he had befriended Roy, George, and him. Over the following few weeks Alex had told the men about the silver mine in Timmins and how if they invested early, they would easily treble their money within the year. It had all sounded so plausible at the time, indeed everything about the consortium appeared foolproof.

Alex had said that there was a limited window of opportunity for investors and if they were interested, they should act with expediency. So that was how their little consortium had been formed. Legal shareholder's certificates were produced, signed, and witnessed by Alex's lawyer and then Roy and George had died. Tom showed Rose the shareholders certificate highlighting Section 12 and George's cautionary note about Alex.

"You see, love, I've been trying to get hold of Alex as I want to have a long talk to him, but he seems to have disappeared off the face of the earth."

"But surely, Tom, you know where he lives?" Rose said trying hard to keep her voice steady.

"Yes, well, he told us that he lived on Tuyll Street, but he never actually gave us his address. I don't know where everybody lives in our Thirsty Thursday's group, you know, I don't even know half their surnames. I'm sure that it's the same with you and your Mah-jong friends.

"You get introduced to someone normally by their first name and that's how it was with Alex. Anyway, I've been making enquiries and asking around, no one seems to know where he's gone. The thing is, love, I don't believe that Roy and George's deaths were accidental. Oh, I know that it would be really difficult to prove otherwise, but the way I see it, I'm next on the list."

"Oh, Tom, this all sounds a bit far-fetched and melodramatic. I'm sure that there's a simple explanation for Alex's absence and I'm also fairly convinced that the shareholders agreement is pretty standard in consortiums, although I would have thought that the spouses would automatically inherit the shares."

"I thought so too but when I asked Henry to look through

the shareholders agreement, he said that it was all there in writing and was perfectly legal."

"Who is Henry? Honestly, Tom, you seem to know an awful lot of strange men."

"I play golf with Henry every now and then and for your information he is a retired lawyer and not 'strange' at all."

Rose nodded her head and let out a deep sigh.

"So, Tom, can you not just sell your shares to Alex and get your money back?"

Tom looked at Rose with a great deal of exasperation. "Yes, of course I would like to do that but in order to do so I would have to talk to Alex, and we're back to square one."

His voice had risen considerably, and Rose could see the stress building up in eyes. She decided to change the subject.

"Oh, by the way, Jessica just called. She wants us to meet them half-way in Kingston to save them driving all the way from Montreal. I said that it would be an awful lot of travelling for us to do in one day. Maybe we could book an Airbnb in Kingston or Gananoque. What do you think?"

"Yes, that would work. I'll go on to the Airbnb site and see what I can find."

Good, Rose thought. It would take his mind off Alex and all his fanciful thoughts of murder. Rose did, however, feel somewhat alarmed. George and Roy's deaths had occurred so close to each other and both were supposedly accidents. It all just seemed rather too coincidental and if there was one thing Rose did not believe in it was coincidences. It was time to speak to her friend Susan, retired DCI Parker, currently happily abiding at the Harbour Court condos in Bayfield. Rose picked up the phone and tapped in Susan's number.

Susan had just emerged from the hot tub which had been

her retirement present to herself. She was standing stark naked in the living room, a towel in one hand and a glass of wine in the other. Glancing at the clock on the dining room wall, Susan was alarmed to see that it was already past twelve. She was supposed to be meeting Ian Green at one in Goderich. Her telephone rang just as she was about to go upstairs to have a shower. It was Rose Blair, her good friend.

"Hi, Susan. Are you free for coffee? I've got to talk to you about something Tom's got involved in and we need your advice. Are you free this afternoon?"

"Oh, Rose, I'm having a lunch date with Ian, but I'll be back in the village by about three. Why don't I give you a call when I get home and then we can get together and talk about Tom. I have to say you've got me intrigued."

Rose suddenly remembered the croquet social.

"Oh, blast, I forgot, I'm actually tied up this afternoon. Oh, it will have to wait until tomorrow. What are you doing tomorrow morning?"

"Well, after my run I've got nothing planned until the evening. Why don't you come over here about ten?"

"That's great. Okay, I'll see you tomorrow morning. Now can we get back to your lunch date. Did you say you were having lunch with Ian Green? Do you mean the pathologist from Goderich, the one with the egg farm down Porter's Line?"

"Umm...yes, Doctor Ian Green, but he doesn't own the egg farm, it's his mom's; he lives with her and helps with the farm as well as being the county pathologist."

"Oh, Susan, you kept this quiet. When did you two get together? I know that he's fancied you for ages but how did he finally pluck up the courage to ask you out?"

Susan laughed, "Oh, Rose, we literally bumped into each other in Food Basics a couple of weeks ago and we chatted like old friends. Then we went for coffee to Cate's Café and now he's invited me to lunch and that's as far as we've got. But you know something, I really like him. He's honest and gentle and really old fashioned in his ways."

"Oh, wow, do I see romance in the air?" Rose laughed. It was time that her dear friend found true love. Her disastrous marriage, all but very brief, to Tonne, had ended a couple of years ago and her divorce was now final. Yes, it was time for her to find love again.

"Right, well, I'm standing here with absolutely nothing on and I have to make myself beautiful for my date so I'm going now, Rose. See you tomorrow."

THREE

That evening after a pleasant afternoon of tea and croquet, Rose had cooked Tom's favourite meal of beef-cobbler with mashed potatoes and sweet corn, followed by apple crisp and cream. For a short while Tom had lost his hang-dog expression and appeared relaxed and back to his old self.

When they had cleared away the dishes, loaded the dishwasher, and generally tidied up the kitchen, Tom announced that he would take the dogs for a short walk. Ben and Puff, their beloved dogs were both getting up in their years and could no longer manage long walks or, indeed the stairs in Pioneer Park that led down to the beach.

"Don't go too far, Tom, poor Ben's back legs are quite weak."

"Don't worry, love, I'll be gentle with the old boy. I won't be long, back soon."

It was a beautiful June evening. The air was fresh and the sky a clear azure blue. Sunset would be around 8:45 p.m., an hour away. Tom walked down Bayfield Terrace along to Pioneer Park, stopping regularly to allow Puff and Ben to have a good sniff and to leave their own mark for other dogs to smell. Looking out over the lake Tom counted five sailing boats enjoying the gentle breeze. He should take *Tranquillity* out for a sail, Tom thought, although there was a little voice in his head saying that maybe it was time that he sold his boat as he rarely had time for sailing these days, particularly after taking on the business of looking after Rose's sister's cottage. Had they known that it would be such hard work they probably would never have agreed to meet and greet and tidy up after the guests. Maybe, after the summer season was over, they would talk to Kate about finding someone else to manage the house.

"Come on Puff and Ben, time to walk home." Tom pulled at their leashes and headed back towards Bayfield Terrace. They were halfway down the road when Tom first spotted the dark grey Lincoln Navigator. It appeared to be going rather fast and heading directly towards him. Tom yanked at the dog's leashes and jumped onto the grass verge dragging the dogs as he stumbled and fell onto the grass with the two dogs on top of him.

"What the hell was that all about?" Tom muttered to himself as slowly realization hit him; someone had just tried to run him over, someone driving a big arse Lincoln Navigator. But who would want him out of the way? Of course, Alex would become the total shareholder of the consortium if Tom wasn't around. But surely that was just a little too far-fetched to think that Alex would systematically eliminate all three shareholders just to gain total control. They were, after all, only minor investors in the big scheme of things. It all seemed too bizarre. Tom knew that if he went to the police they would never believe him, besides, they would have to track Alex down and Tom had already found that his friend had disappeared without a trace. He walked back home feeling the dark shadow of depression, mixed with fear, begin to consume him.

Rose looked up from reading her book when the dogs came charging in followed by a very subdued looking husband.

"What's wrong, Tom? You look as if you've seen a ghost."

"Someone tried to kill me just now, love. I'm fairly convinced that I'm on Alex's hit list. I actually feared for my life back there."

"Good God, Tom, sit down and I'll get you a drink. This is getting serious, and I don't like it one single bit."

Rose poured Tom a stiff whisky and went to sit beside him on the sofa.

"Don't worry, darling, nobody's going to get you because we'll make sure that you can't be found. From now on you're going to lay low."

Tom nodded and closed his eyes. Rose would help protect him; he just knew it.

Sitting in Susan's cosy living room sipping coffee and listening to the chorus of birds chirping away outside in the trees behind the condos, Rose could almost believe that everything was right in the world. Susan came into the room carrying a plate of muffins.

"Before you say anything, Rose, I did not bake them myself, they're from the Mennonite market down the road. Now, tell me what's bugging you. I can see that you're agitated."

Rose put her coffee down and cleared her throat before

beginning to tell Susan all about Tom's reckless investment and the subsequent accidental deaths of Roy and George.

"And last night Tom was almost run over by a big beast of a car. He's convinced that he's going to be next on the list and I tend to agree with him."

"But surely Tom's tried to talk to this Alex, hasn't he? He is obviously the key to all of this. They need to have a serious talk the two of them."

"Yes, well I said the same thing to Tom, but it appears that Alex has disappeared without a trace. He's done a runner."

Susan was thoughtful. "Nobody can totally disappear, Rose, there are ways to track people down, but I do agree that Tom needs to get away and lay low for a while. Look, I have a family cottage up in the Muskokas. He could hole himself down there for a week while we try to find Alex. The other line that I would like to follow is the Silvercorp mine. I'll do a bit of research and see what comes up. You and I might even take a little road trip and go and check it out ourselves. How does that sound to you?"

"Wow, that all sounds so positive and great. Thank you, Susan, I can always rely on you to come up with a plan. Now tell me all about your date with Ian Green?"

Susan laughed lightly and poured herself another cup of coffee from the French Press on the table.

"Well, there's not much really to tell. We met at Thyme on 21 and had an excellent meal. Ian's a good conversationalist and because I was in the police force for so many years and understand his line of work, he was able to chat easily about some of his cases, a few of which I remember from my days at the Serious Crimes Unit in London. Talking of which, how are things going with your sister and that handsome DCI Hargreaves?"

Rose paused for thought before answering. "Oh, Susan, she seems so happy and I'm thrilled for her. She got a job at Labatt's Brewery in charge of the tasting room so it's a bit like working at The Albion which she used to love. It seems that Rachel, John's daughter, has taken a shine to her too, so everything couldn't be better."

Susan looked at her friend intently before saying, "And what about you, Rose? How do you really feel about it all?"

Rose laughed, "You know me too well, Susan. I can't deny that I felt a tad jealous of my sister to begin with, but then a great sense of relief washed over me because, you see, being attracted to John really played hard on my emotions and I could never betray Tom, so it's all been for the best in the long run."

"Well, for your sake, Rose, I really hope that you have got over your attraction to John otherwise that could pose a big problem between you and your sister."

"Oh, don't I know it. No, that's a phase of my life I feel distinctly mortified about, but life has a way of putting everything into perspective and I really feel that Tom and I have come out even stronger and hopefully, wiser. That's why seeing Tom so unhappy now is breaking my heart. I need to get to the bottom of this scam and soon. What about the fraud squad, Susan?"

Susan looked pensive before answering. "The trouble is, Rose, Alex has technically done nothing wrong in the eyes of the law. If it clearly states in the shareholders agreement that all shares automatically get passed to the remaining shareholders, then that makes it perfectly legal.

"The Silvercorp company obviously has a good lawyer. Now, as to the accidental deaths and the attempt made on Tom's life well, that too would be very hard to prove without any witnesses. I do, however, wonder why anyone would go as far as to murder just to gain some shares. It's not that they're worth millions, is it?"

"I know Susan, it does beg the question just what are the shares really worth? The only way we're going to find out is by digging, excuse the pun, into the mine and its ownership. A road trip is getting more and more likely if you're sure that you're up to it."

"If Tom goes up to the cottage, he could take the dogs with him and I'll get my neighbour Gina to keep an eye on Fluffy, so that only leaves the question, when should we leave?"

Rose mulled it over for a bit trying to remember when the next set of Airbnb guests were due to check-in at her sister's cottage. Also, Abby and Ella were scheduled to visit them in ten days. They would have to depart in the next couple of days, Rose thought.

With their trip planned for two days ahead, Rose left Susan suddenly galvanized into action. She would go to Goderich and do a big shop. If Tom was going to be away for a week, he would need provisions. Susan and she would go on the fly, check into motels, eat out, and stay away for however long it took to get some answers from the mine.

Tom, in the meantime, continued his quest to find Alex. He emailed all his pals from the Thirsty Thursday's group asking if anyone had Alex's contact details. He also went back three months in his emails to see if he could find any communication between either Alex, George, or Roy. This drew another blank. Feeling thoroughly frustrated Tom decided to walk to

the Albion, maybe having a pint might clear his head. Leaving
Puff and Ben behind he walked over to Louisa Street and was
halfway when he spotted what looked like the same Lincoln
Navigator that had tried to run him down the previous
evening. It was parked outside the house of one of Rose's
friends.

If Alex were the owner of the car that would mean that he
was acquainted with Rose's friend. Tom decided to go for his
pint, but to call in to visit Rose's friend on his way home. He
was just second guessing his decision and thinking that he
should probably just go and knock on the door and see if Alex
was there when the decision was taken away from him. The
large Lincoln accelerated past him and had disappeared before
Tom could react. But was it Alex behind the wheel?

Rose staggered into the house, both arms laden with shopping bags. Trying to work her way to the kitchen was like
walking through a minefield with Ben and Puff jumping up
with excitement weaving in and out of her legs, just so pleased
to see her.

Tom was nowhere to be found so Rose busied herself with
putting everything away. She was just about to make herself a
cup of tea when the telephone rang. It was their daughter
Anne.

"Oh, hi Mom, I'm in London at Western University
attending a conference. It finishes today and I've got a few days
spare, I just wondered if I could pop over tomorrow for a visit.
I'm staying with Paul and Atsuko and he said that he would
drive us both over to Bayfield, if that's okay by you?"

Anne and her husband, Alan, had split up the previous
year after Alan had been found in a compromising position
with their nanny. They had moved to Toronto from Halifax

after Anne had been offered a head of department position at Ryerson College. Alan had retired from his position at Dalhousie as senior professor of the Astrophysics department. Now, after his reckless affair, they lived in separate apartments, but in the same condo block down on Harbour Front in Toronto. They shared looking after the children and, so far, the arrangement appeared to be working.

"Yes, I'm free tomorrow and it will be lovely to see Paul and you again. You'll stay for lunch I presume?"

"Oh, yes Mom that would be great. So, we'll see you around twelve, okay?"

"Right, see you tomorrow, darling, safe travelling."

Rose put the phone down and proceeded to fill the kettle for the much-needed cup of tea. She was just pouring the boiling water into the tea pot when Tom appeared. He came over to her and planted a kiss on her cheeks. His breath smelt of beer, *no guesses as to where he'd been*, Rose thought, but Tom was excited and agitated too.

"Love, I saw that vehicle again, you know, the one that tried to mow me down yesterday. It was parked outside your friend Carolyn's house. I've just been there but they must have gone out as no one came to the door. Maybe you could call her and ask if she knows Alex?"

"Yes, of course I'll do that, but I've got some news for you too. I met with Susan and she agrees that you should lay low and she's offered you her family cottage up near Bracebridge in the Muskoka's. She says that you can hide up there for a while. In the meantime, we're going to do some investigating ourselves. Tom, I really think that you should go sooner rather than later. Look, you can take the dogs with you for company.

Susan suggests that you leave tonight or early tomorrow morning and just make sure that you're not followed."

Tom looked at Rose with amazement. "You two have really been scheming, haven't you? Yes, you're right, I can't live watching over my shoulder all the time, I'll go and pack my bags and gather stuff to bring with me. I'm only going to stay for a week, so I hope that you and Susan can make some headway in sorting out this whole sorry business."

FOUR

The next morning after their cup of tea in bed, Tom got dressed and calling the dogs, he grabbed his hold-all, kissed Rose goodbye, and quietly left their house. It was 7:00 a.m.

It would take almost four hours to reach the cottage which was nestled by the water's edge on Healey Lake, just twenty minutes outside of Bracebridge. Tom drove carefully, keeping his eyes on the rear mirror just to make sure that no one was following him. As there was little traffic on the road he didn't stop until he reached Mount Forest, where he pulled into a Tim Horton's. Taking the dogs leashes, he clipped them on and took them for a short walk before going into the coffee shop and ordering his breakfast. Tom looked at his watch, it was only 8:30 a.m.; he had made really good time and at that rate would be in the Muskoka's before mid-day.

Travelling on Highway 89 he finally reached the 400 having travelled through Alliston and Cookstown. Traffic on the 400 was relatively light until approaching Barrie where road work seemed to be holding up the traffic. Tom sighed. He had been doing so well time wise until Barrie and now an extra half hour had been added. Soon, however, he was able to get off the 400 and onto Highway 11, he was able to make up the lost time as the road was almost empty.

The scenery had changed as he reached the vast Canadian Shield. Now huge granite blocks dotted the hilly terrain which lay heavily with birch and conifer trees. Tom stopped again just outside Gravenhurst, once more taking the dogs for a quick walk and grabbing a coffee and donut at Tim Horton's.

After taking the exit from Highway 11 just south of Bracebridge, he finally reached the end of the asphalt and turned onto a dirt road at a sign for Healey Lake. Once Tom was off the main roads, the gravel roadway twisted and turned through the muskeg and bush. It was like navigating a rabbit warren with little side-lanes going off at strange angles and banks of small wooden signs at each intersection with names of cottage owners pointing in the different directions.

Tom eventually found the Parkers cottage and drove down a very steep driveway descending to a lovely house nestled amongst tall pine trees literally on the side of the lake. Ben and Puff were thrilled to be free of the car and they charged without hesitation straight down to the lake. Susan had warned Tom that bears and porcupines frequented the property. He should be careful when barbequing and make sure that he secured the garbage bins so that bears and raccoons couldn't open them; he should also be mindful of Puff and Ben with the pesky porcupines.

Tom remembered the damage the porcupines had caused at his friend Doug's cottage on Manitoulin Island. He had never realized that porcupines could chew through wood so recklessly.

All in all, he had made excellent time. He would call Rose and let her know that he was safely ensconced at the cottage on Healey Lake.

Soon after Rose had spoken to Tom, Paul and Anne pulled up outside their house. Rose had decided that the three of them would go out for lunch. She would let them decide where to go as at this time of the year they wouldn't have to make reservations.

The front door burst open, and Anne rushed in followed by Paul. Rose's spirits lifted as Anne hugged her. Her daughter was like a breath of fresh air and Rose laughed with the sheer pleasure of having her two children with her again, it was just a shame that Jessica couldn't have joined them too, but she would at least be seeing their oldest daughter soon. *I am truly blessed*, Rose thought, for the millionth time, blessed with family that she so loved.

"Mom, where's Dad?" Anne asked while putting the kettle on to make some coffee.

Rose had decided not to tell Paul and Anne about Tom's problems. They would only worry.

"Oh, your dad has gone up to the Muskokas for a short holiday."

Anne looked at her mother strangely, "You mean to say he's gone there by himself? Why didn't you go with him?"

Paul glanced at his sister catching the alarm in her voice. "Are you and Dad alright, Mom?" Paul asked frown lines creasing his handsome forehead.

"Of course we're alright." Rose laughed trying not to sound

indignant. "Sometimes even old people need their own space, darling."

Anne and Paul looked incredulous.

"But you've never gone away without each other, Mom, have you?"

Anne was like a dog with an old bone, she would not let it go easily, but Rose was determined to keep her silence.

"Now enough about your father, look, we're going to go out for lunch and I want you to decide where. Come on, we'll have some coffee and then go and get something to eat."

They had just taken their coffees into the sunroom when the phone rang. It was Susan.

"Rose, has Tom arrived at the cottage safely?"

"Yes, I was going to call you, but Paul and Anne have just arrived. I was meaning to let Tom know that we would be heading up north tomorrow. Did you find anything about Silvercorp?"

"Yes, quite a lot, but I'll tell you all about it on our way up to Timmins tomorrow. I'd like to leave around six as it's a good eight hours away and we should get there before the mine closes at five. Pack clothes enough for a couple of days away and we'll check into a motel when we get to the mine. Okay, see you tomorrow."

"Mom," Anne called, "Who were you talking to? Did I hear you say that you were heading up north tomorrow? Who are you going with? Mom, just what is going on?"

"There is nothing going on and if you really want to know, your father is at my friend Susan Parker's family cottage on Healey Lake and that was actually Susan on the phone right now talking to me."

Rose wanted to tell her daughter to mind her own business, but she didn't want to cause an argument so she bit her tongue and said no more. Anne, however, was determined to have the last word.

"Well, I think it's most strange and not at all like Dad to bugger off without you. I still think that something's going on here, don't you, Paul?"

Paul had kept quiet throughout and now looked decidedly uncomfortable. He did, however, also think that Tom's absence was a bit strange. "Yeah, well, maybe Dad needed a break from Mom."

Rose was about to retort when Anne snorted, "More like Mom needs a break from Dad, you dork. Look, Mom, have you and Dad had a falling out? Oh my God, he hasn't run off with anyone else, has he?"

Rose laughed out loud. "Now Anne, you're letting your imagination run away with yourself. How many times do I have to say that your father and I are just fine? Right, have you chosen a restaurant yet? I'm getting hungry."

Anne was still not mollified. "Well, Uncle Bob went off with Aunty Kate's best friend, didn't he and he was old like Dad."

"Now Anne, enough is enough, just drop the subject will you. I want to have a nice lunch with you both and catch up with all your news, so let's be going into the village. As you haven't decided on a restaurant, I'll choose for you, and I choose The Black Dog."

Suddenly Anne wailed, "Where are Puff and Ben, Mom? I haven't seen them since we arrived."

"They went with your father, darling." Before Anne could say anything, Rose marched to the front door and headed out of the house with Paul and Anne running to catch up.

During their excellent meal, Rose left Paul and Anne to go to the washroom. As soon as she was out of ear shot, Anne said to Paul, "I'm not buying this crap about Dad needing his own space. Since when has Dad needed his own space? I think that we need to go and talk to him. Are you free tomorrow, Paul?"

Paul taught ESL at Fanshawe College in London and it being June meant that he was on holiday until September. Atsuko, his wife, however, may not take kindly to him disappearing off for a few days particularly as she was stuck at home with Yuki, who was three, and baby Midori. He would have to text her and see what she had to say."

"It will depend on Atsuko. I'll text her and see what she says. What about you? I thought that you were attending a conference at Western?"

"Yes, well I've sat in on the major part of the conference and I won't be missed if I don't show up tomorrow. Allan is looking after the kids so I'm free for two days. I really would like to get to the bottom of this, Paul. You know I won't rest until I know what's going on."

Rose returned to the table and smiled at her children. "Is everything alright? You both look so serious."

"Everything's cool, Mom." Paul said. He had just sent Atsuko a text message and was waiting to hear back from her.

They finished off their lunch and were about to walk home when Rose spotted Jean, George's widow, who was standing outside The Purple Peony as if waiting for someone.

"Umm...Paul and Anne, you go ahead. I'm just going to pop across the road to have a word with a friend. I'll be right behind you in a few minutes."

Paul and Anne nodded okay and watched as their mother rushed across the road to where an older woman was standing.

"Oh well, this gives us the opportunity to talk, doesn't it Paul. Have you heard back from Atsuko yet?"

Paul was looking at his phone as Anne was speaking. He glanced at his sister and gave her the thumbs up sign.

"I guess we're going on a road trip together, sis. If we leave soon, we'll be up in the Muskoka's before it gets dark. Let's hot foot it back to Mom's and make a pot of tea, then leave as soon as she gets back. The big question is, are we going to tell Mom where we're going or not?"

Anne looked at her brother as if he's lost his mind. "Of course we're not going to tell Mom. She'd be on the phone straight away to tell Dad that we were on our way. No, we want to catch him unaware and then we can grill him about what's really going on."

"Okay. I get it. Right, let's get going."

The two of them set off at quite a pace leaving Rose chatting to Jean who looked to be in a great deal of distress.

Jean dabbed her eyes with a paper tissue. She had tried hard to staunch her tears, but to no avail. Rose's heart went out to her friend. She gave her a big hug and asked her how she was doing. Between little sobs Jean managed to answer.

"The trouble is, Rose, everyone's been so kind and there is something about people being just too kind. Every time someone tells me how sorry they are my eyes well up and it's like picking at an old scab, the soreness keeps bleeding again and again. Anyway, I did want to talk to you about Alex.

"I looked at the shareholders agreement and in the small print it says that all shares automatically get passed on to the existing shareholders. Does that mean that both Eileen and my shares go to Tom and Alex? That's a mighty lot of money to forfeit. I would have thought that Tom and Alex would have to buy the shares off us, don't you think that would make more sense?"

Rose felt decidedly uncomfortable and she understood exactly what Jean was getting at, after all $200,000 was an enormous amount of money to most people. She didn't quite know what to say.

Jean plowed on. "I can't speak for Eileen, but I know that George was thinking about buying her shares and now he too is dead and I'm $200,000 short with nothing to show for it. Something doesn't add up, Rose. It's nothing short of a scam and somehow our sensible, loving husbands fell for it all; hook, line, and sinker."

With that said Jean burst into a fresh bout of tears again saying in a thick voice, "I'm sorry, Rose, I'm sorry."

Rose had always been a real sucker for tears as she tended to cry with anyone who had tears in their eyes, she just couldn't help herself and that day was no exception. She brushed the back of her hand over her wet eyes and took a big gulp of air. Hugging Jean, she broke away and bade her goodbye and quickly scuttled away as fast as she could.

Paul and Anne were waiting for their mother with a pot of tea already brewed and carried through into the sunroom.

"So, Mom, after tea we're going to head out. We've both got tons to do."

Rose looked surprised. "Are you sure, darlings? I thought that you would like to go to the beach or something like that?"

Paul and Anne looked at each other and then Anne said quickly, "No, Mom, we both have loads to do. Look, I'd like to bring Ollie and Millie down for a few days soon, if that would be okay? They haven't been to Bayfield since Easter and now that summer is finally here, beach time beckons. I'll call you and we can set something up."

"We have Abby and Ella here for the week after next. It would be lovely for them to see their cousins. Maybe you could bring them down then?"

"That sounds like a plan, Mom. Now Paul, are you ready to hit the road?"

Rose smiled, Anne had always been bossy, although Jessica got the prize for assertiveness. Paul generally had let his sisters order him about until even he, on the odd occasion, had lashed out and stubbornly refused to acquiesce.

Paul hugged his mother and gave her a big kiss and Anne followed suit. Soon the house was quiet, too quiet without Tom and the dogs, Rose thought as she tidied up the teacups and brought the tray into the kitchen. She decided to give Susan a call.

"Hi, Susan. Paul and Anne have just left and it's awfully quiet here. Do you fancy coming around for supper and then we can plan our next few days?"

Susan agreed and then Rose thought, *What on earth am I going to cook for dinner?*

Opening the fridge, she immediately saw the left over chicken. There were always vegetables, milk, and eggs and the basics: rice, pasta, and potatoes. She would steer away from a pasta dish as Susan had spent a year in Italy and had probably superior cooking skills in the pasta department. Rose pulled the chicken out of the fridge and started to chop up the cooked meat. She would make a chicken pie and serve it with mashed potatoes, broccoli, and a nice, fresh salad- *pure comfort food,* Rose thought.

. . .

SUSAN ARRIVED CARRYING a bottle of wine and a box of chocolates. Rose heard the distinctive rumbling sound of Susan's Porsche as she turned into their drive. The sleek silver Porsche had been another of her retirement presents to herself: the hot tub being the first present which now sat squarely in her small courtyard in Harbour Court, a testimony to her thirty years of service to the police force.

Rose opened the door and welcomed her friend giving Susan a warm hug as she took the wine and chocolates from her.

"Yum, we'll have these for dessert. Come on through to the sunroom, we'll have some drinks there before eating our dinner."

Rose led Susan through their cosy living room and into the light and modern sun lounge. The contrast between the two rooms was quite extreme Susan thought as she sat down on a rattan loveseat and looked around at the modern art hung on the end wall and the glass desk in the corner. She knew that Rose had been working on decluttering, but this minimalist look was not warm and fuzzy at all. Thank goodness the main living room still felt like Rose and Tom's house. Rose had observed her friend looking around the sunroom.

"So, what do you think? What about this picture, I bought it from Main Street Gallery last week? Tell me truthfully, do you like it?"

Susan didn't quite know what to say. "Well... I'm not sure what I'm looking at? I love the colours, but is it just made up of triangles and squares or am I missing something?"

Rose laughed, "Oh, Susan, you sound just like Tom. It's modern abstract art. I wanted a big splash of colour on the wall to brighten up the room. I love it."

"Well, then, that's all that counts. You certainly have decluttered. What did you do with all your rugs and lamps? Umm... it does look a little bit austere in here."

"Yes, Paul and Anne said the same thing. They suggested that I buy loads of plants. What do you think?"

"Yes, some indoor plants would probably do the trick. Right, let's have a drink. By the way, something most certainly smells delicious."

Rose smiled as she went to open a bottle of wine, "We've got chicken pie for dinner tonight. Now, Susan, did you manage to contact your friend at the Fraud Squad?"

"Yes, I did, and he ran Alex's name through the system and there were no red-flags so he's off the radar and, of course, this could be his first scam in which case there would be no record yet. I did ask my friend to run a credit card check and no one of that name came up; likewise, no evidence of an Alex Boychuk on EMPAC records but, of course, he might have been renting so I tried Canada 911, and nothing came up.

"You know, Rose, most people use cell phones so 911 isn't as good as it used to be in tracking people down. The other thing my friend in the Fraud Squad said is that in all likelihood Alex Boychuk is not his real name so we're barking up the wrong tree even trying to track him down. Our best plan of action is what we're going to be doing and that is visiting the mine in person. I'd like to bet we'll find all our answers there including the identity of our mysterious Alex Boychuk."

Rose was quiet for a while and then she finally said, "Don't you think, Susan, that we might be going on a wild goose chase?"

"No, we have to get to the bottom of this, Rose, otherwise Tom will be permanently looking over his shoulder and, besides your friends, Jean and Eileen, have been duped out of $200,000. There should be some recourse for action."

"Yes, of course, but how will we even begin to get the money paid back if the shares were all legal. Honestly, it's the men's fault for not reading the small print, surely?"

"Well, you're right on that one. What possessed Tom and his friends to enter into that consortium without first seeking legal advice? Any lawyer worth their salt would have pointed out the small print and Section 12. At the very least there should have been a buy-out clause. This Alex must have been very persuasive, as most conmen are I suppose. No, we'll sort this out Rose, don't worry. Oh, I also made a call to a good friend of mine who lives in Timmins.

He's the chief OPP officer. I gave him the low down on Alex Boychuk and the silver mine consortium. He said that Silvercorp is totally legit and is one of the areas biggest employers. He told me to tread lightly as absolutely no one would want to see the mine closed down again for whatever reason. On the other hand, Trevor, that's my friend, is more than happy to be on stand-by if we need any help."

"That's brilliant, Susan. Hopefully, we won't need to call him, but it makes me happier knowing that someone has our backs covered. Now, I'm just going to call Tom and then we should both have an early night if we're to leave by six. By the way, I looked at MapQuest and it says nine hours and fifteen minutes, not eight as you said."

Susan laughed, "Ah, but in my Porsche it's much faster. Don't look so shocked, yes, I'm driving and taking my lovely car."

Rose sighed, she knew when she was beaten, but the

thought of eight hours of Susan's driving quite unnerved her. Oh well, she would just have to grin and bare it, that's all.

"Right, I'll be off now. Thanks for the lovely dinner, Rose. Oh, pack your bag for a few days."

"Yes, I do have to be back by the weekend as we have Airbnb guests checking in on Friday at Kate's cottage. Okay, see you tomorrow."

Susan left and once again the house felt too quiet for Rose's liking. She quickly loaded the dishwasher and tidied up the kitchen before making her phone call to Tom.

FIVE

Up in the Muskoka's, Tom was having a terrible time trying to get the smell of skunk out of Ben's fur. He had let both dogs out to wander around the property and a while later Ben had returned absolutely stinking of skunk. The first thing Tom did was to tie Ben up outside while shooing Puff inside. The whiff of skunk could be smelt everywhere. *Right,* Tom thought, *I'll have to bathe Ben in tomato juice,* but he would need an awful lot of it to make a dent on his thick fur.

"Okay, boy, stay here while I drive to the nearest store. Hopefully, I'll be able to purchase some cans of tomato juice, but where would the nearest shop be located?"

In the end, Tom drove into Bracebridge and found a Metro Supermarket. While he was there, he picked up some snacks and beer. He might as well enjoy his enforced holiday while he could. Grabbing four large cans of tomato juice Tom loaded his shopping trolley and wheeled it over to the cashier at the check-out. He was just about to carry his provisions out to the car when he noticed a large black Lincoln Navigator cruising down the street. Surely it couldn't be Alex? Tom thought as he hid behind a pillar on the exit side of Metro where all the trolleys were stored. *If it was Alex,* Tom thought, *does that mean that he followed me here or is it just a coincidence?*

What if he'd placed some sort of GPS tracking devise on his car or something like that? Tom was undecided as to what to do. If there was a tracking devise he would be toast. Maybe he should park his car on a side street and take a taxi or an Uber to Healy Lake. That sounded like the best plan and so he pulled out his phone, opened his Uber app, and found that there was a couple of available cars based in Bracebridge. Having dealt with that he walked quickly to his car and drove off out of the car park and up a hill to what looked like a pleasant neighbourhood. He parked his car in front of one of the houses, pulled out his phone, and booked a locally based Uber driver. Ten minutes later he was sitting in a Toyota Prius, shopping provisions next to him, enjoying being chauffeured to the cottage. Just as the car pulled away, Tom spotted the Lincoln Navigator again. Anxiously he asked the driver to pull over. He looked in the rear mirror and noticed that the Lincoln had also pulled over. Tom spoke urgently to the driver.

"Look, I've got someone tracking me, I thought that it was my car but now I'm not so sure."

The driver interrupted Tom abruptly. "Mate, it's your cellphone. My advice, for what it's worth, is to take the SIM card out and throw it away. Anyone can track someone with a Smart phone as there is a built in GPS system."

Tom looked at the driver with amazement as he reached for his cell phone. Turning it over in his hands he couldn't for the life of him see how he could locate the SIM card, let alone remove it. The Uber driver chuckled to himself.

"I can see, mate, that you haven't a clue. Hand it here and I'll see what I can do."

Tom gave his phone to the driver and watched as he grabbed a paper clip from his clipboard, straightened out one end and proceeded to poke it into a small hole on the side of the phone. He then slid the back off and retrieved the tiny SIM card. Holding it up to Tom he said, "I presume that you don't want this baby?"

Tom shook his head as the driver snapped it in two and tossed the pieces out of the window. "Now, how about we do a quick run around to lose your tail before heading out to Healy Lake?"

They sped away taking a quick right turn and then a left before feeding back into the town traffic on Main Street. Tom looked anxiously in the rear mirror. There was no sign of the Lincoln Navigator.

"Phew, thank you so much. Now let's get to my cottage."

Ten minutes later they pulled up outside the steep driveway to Susan's cottage. Tom could hear the dogs barking like crazy and he swore that he could also smell skunk. Paying the Uber driver a large tip, Tom carried his provisions into the house, pulled out the cans of tomato juice and proceeded to carry them out to where Ben had been tethered.

"Come on old boy, let's get rid of this stinky smell."

Tom poured the tomato juice directly over Ben's fur and began to rub it in. He was almost finished working his way through Ben's coat when a red Mazda pulled up into his driveway and to his amazement, Paul and Anne jumped out. What on earth were his son and daughter doing here? Tom thought as he straightened his back and walked towards his children.

"Phew, what a skunky smell." Paul exclaimed while Anne fanned the air in front of her nose saying, "Yuk, I presume Ben was sprayed by a skunk, Dad?"

Tom nodded his head, "What are you two doing here?"

Paul looked at Anne and Anne looked at Paul, neither of them spoke for a minute.

"Has the cat got your tongues? Tell me, is everything okay, are you bearers of some awful news? Come on, spit it out you two."

Paul finally said, "We visited Mom in Bayfield and she told us that you had come here by yourself for a week as you needed your own space. Look Dad, Mom sounded evasive and thoroughly got us worried. Are you alright? Are Mom and you okay?"

Tom stood there speechless. His own kids were worried enough to drive all this distance to see their father. It really was quite amazing, but what should he tell them? He decided that the only way to go was to tell them the whole sorry truth.

"Let me finish cleaning Ben and then we'll sit down and I'll tell you everything. Maybe one of you could put the kettle on for a nice pot of coffee."

An hour later, the three of them were sitting on the cottage deck feeling quite a mixture of emotions. On the one hand both Paul and Anne had lambasted their father for his foolishness with the consortium and his lack of transparency with their mother. Anne had hotly said, "If I was Mom, I would have cheerfully killed you for investing so much money without consulting me. Honestly, Dad, how could you have done that? It's sneaky and so underhanded."

Tom looked abashed and then Paul had come to his defence. "I suppose you thought you would make a quick killing on the profits of the shares. I get it, but you still should have told Mom, but I'm more concerned about your safety. Surely you should have gone to the police?"

"Your mother spoke to Susan Parker, you know, the retired DCI Serious Crimes officer and she looked at the shareholders certificates. They are apparently perfectly legal. Regarding George and Roy's deaths, Susan said that unless there had been witnesses to say otherwise, their deaths would be considered accidents and nothing more. Susan and your mother are going to drive up to the mine and speak to the owners. Oh, that reminds me, I should give your mother a call as she will be worried if she doesn't hear from me."

Tom reached into his pocket and pulled out his phone and it was only then that he realized that it wouldn't work. There was no SIM card.

SIX

Susan picked Rose up bang on six o'clock the next morning. It was a beautiful summer's day, the temperature already twenty degrees so early in the morning. The air felt fresh and clear, humidity levels were low, and the sun had already risen on the horizon. Rose felt quite excited to be going on a little road trip with Susan. A change of scenery would do her good and having the company of her good friend for the duration of the journey would be refreshing. The two friends had known each other for years, had gone to college together, shared the same digs in Kingston and had even got married the same year. However, Susan's marriage to the jerk had barely lasted five years whereas Tom and Rose had now been together for almost forty-five years. Susan had changed careers after her divorce deciding that teaching was not her vocation, instead she had chosen the police force and had to really work hard as a woman to get anywhere. She had, by sheer hard work and tenacity, made her way up the career ladder to ultimately the role of DCI of the Serious Crimes Unit in London, Ontario. After the death of her fiancé, Henri Le Brun, a Quebec Sureté Officer, and five years later her disastrous marriage to drugs squad officer, Tony, Susan had retired from the police force and bought a condo on Harbour Court, Bayfield, close to the marina. She had come out of retirement for two years helping Serious Crimes out until they had managed to get a replacement, DCI Hargreaves. Now, Susan was fully retired and loving every minute of it.

Rose picked up her cell phone and tapped in Tom's number. There was no answer. A small frown creased her forehead.

"What's up Rose?" Susan asked.

"It's funny, I tried phoning Tom last night and he didn't answer and now just the same, no answer."

"Oh, I wouldn't worry Rose, knowing Tom he's probably out walking with the dogs and has left his phone behind in the cottage. Call him again when we stop for a break in a couple of hours. By the way, how did your visit with Paul and Anne go?"

"It was all a bit strange. When they found out that Tom had gone off to your cottage on his own they started to grill me. I think that they're convinced that Tom and I have split up or something like that. You see, I didn't want to tell them about the mine consortium and the threat to Tom's life. The kids worry enough as it is without giving them anything else to feed on."

Just then Rose's phone rang. "Oh, that's probably Tom right now." Susan said as she once more put her foot down to accelerate past a large haulage truck. The Porsches' engine roared as Rose gripped her seat and clenched her teeth. Susan drove like a Formula 1 driver, the 400 now was her racetrack.

Rose answered her phone. It was not Tom, but Jessica, their eldest daughter calling from Montreal.

"Mom, I just got a text message from Anne. Are you and Dad really having problems? She said that Dad had left you and gone to stay up in the Muskoka's or something equally weird. Is it true? What's going on, Mom?"

Rose laughed out loud and Susan gave her a queried look. "Oh, darling, of course Dad and I are fine. I think Paul and Anne got the wrong end of the stick. Look, I'll tell you all about it next week, okay?"

"Are we still on for Kingston? Did Dad book an Airbnb, Mom?"

In all the kerfuffle Tom had omitted to book anything. *Oh, well,* Rose thought, they could always just check into a motel.

"Don't worry, darling, it's all in hand, now I must go as I'm in the car with my friend Susan and the reception is a bit spotty. I'll call you in a few days time, alright?"

Rose ended the phone call and let out a big sigh. "Kids, they're always texting each other. They're convinced that we're having marital problems, honestly, just as if, we're rather old for that now."

As the words left her mouth Rose wanted to take them back as she remembered her almost affair with the handsome DCI Hargreaves. *You're never too old for love,* she thought, but didn't say out loud.

Funnily enough, Susan had been thinking along the same lines as her friend finally admitting to herself that her new relationship with Ian Green was beginning to feel more serious. She certainly did not feel too old for love.

The two women drove along in companionable silence until they reached a service station a little north of Barrie just before the fork for Highway 11. Rose was desperate for the washrooms and as soon as they had stopped, she made a dash for the building. Susan went to wait in line at the Tim Horton's booth. Rose soon joined her and they both ordered coffees and bowls of chilli. Rose pulled out her phone and tried ringing Tom again. There was still no answer.

"Now, I'm seriously getting worried." Rose said an anxious look clouding her face.

"I'm sure that there's a logical explanation for it, Rose." Susan said, "Look, I tell you what, why don't you try phoning Paul or Anne, didn't Jessica say something about them heading up to the cottage to talk to their dad?"

"Yes, you're quite right and that's a good idea. I'll text Anne and see if she can shed some light on her father."

After Tom had told Paul and Anne the whole sad story, Anne decided to cook lunch for the three of them. It was while she was chopping up the vegetables that she received Rose's text message.

"Dad," she shouted out the window. Paul and Tom had wandered down to the dock, beer in hands and were deep in conversation. "Dad, it's Mom, she wants to talk to you."

Tom walked quickly back to the house saying, "Do you mind, love?" He took his daughter's phone and tapped in Rose's number. She answered straight away.

"Tom, oh thank God you're alright. I was so worried as I couldn't get in touch with you."

Tom interrupted her, "I had to take the SIM card out of my phone as I was being followed by, I assume, Alex in his Lincoln Navigator. I thought that my car had been fitted with a tracking devise and then my Uber driver said that it was more likely to be my phone. Anyway, the upshot is that I don't have a working cellphone. How are you doing, love? I miss you already and it's only been two days."

Rose had found Tom's garbled conversation strange and she wasn't sure what to think. Was he cracking up or was he just getting paranoid? She decided to humour him.

"So, you don't have a phone now. How are we going to communicate?"

Susan, who had been listening in to Rose and Tom's conversation interrupted them by saying, "Tell Tom to go to a variety store and buy a throw away pay-as-you-go phone. There is no way to trace anyone on those devices."

"Did you hear that, Tom? Susan suggests that you buy one of those cheap pay-as-you-go phones."

"Oh yes, well I suppose I could do that." He said not sounding very enthusiastic, "By the way, love, Paul and Anne are here and Ben got skunked. I've had a terrible time trying to get rid of the smell. Tomato juice definitely does not work."

"Poor you, darling, just try hydrogen peroxide mixed with cider vinegar and liquid soap. Oh, and I knew that Anne and Paul were with you otherwise how would I have called you?"

Rose wondered if Tom had the beginnings of dementia. It worried her as he often repeated himself or couldn't remember what he had just said. *It's probably just that we're getting older,* she told herself, but it was still rather disconcerting.

"So, what have you been up to, love?" Tom said.

"Well, I thought that I told you, Susan and I are driving up to the mine to try to get to the bottom of this mess. We thought where better to start than at the source."

"You mean to say you're on your way there right now, love?"

"Yes, and we're in the Porsche so we're making break-neck

speed. We're on Highway 11, just past the turn off for Orillia. We're going to stop off at Webbers for lunch."

As Rose spoke, she could smell hamburgers cooking. There, ahead of them was the incongruous flyover stretching across the highway connecting the massive car park with the restaurant. It was positively amazing how in twenty years Webbers had grown from a small road stop burger joint to this now multi-million-dollar enterprise.

Susan pulled off the highway and parked her car. The two friends climbed out of the Porsche stretching their arms and legs. Rose eyed the stairway ahead and thought of her painful knee joints. *Oh, well*, she thought, *a bit of exercise will probably do me good, even though my knees may not thank me for it.*

SEVEN

Tom gave Anne's phone back to her and sat down heavily. He didn't feel at all happy at the thought of Susan and Rose driving all that distance to visit Silvercorp.

"Dad, are you alright? You look worried about something?" Paul looked concerned; his father worried him. He appeared to have aged over-night these past few days.

"Yes, I am worried, son. You see your mother and her friend Susan Parker have taken it on themselves to drive up to the mine and confront the management. That greatly concerns me."

"And rightly so, Dad, Mom must be off her head thinking that she can get any rational answers from those crooks. They could be driving into a minefield, excuse the pun. But Dad, we can't let them go alone as it could be very dangerous to say the very least."

"Well, what do you suggest that we do?"

Paul had been studying his phone intently and he looked up and handed his phone to Tom.

"Look, Dad, we're here and if you go back to highway 11 and keep driving, you get eventually to Timmins. Silvercorp mine is here." He pointed to the map on his phone.

"I reckon that if we set off now we could get there by 4:00 p.m. or 5:00 depending on how fast we drive."

"Surely you're not thinking of driving to the mine, Paul," Tom said a note of alarm creeping into his voice.

"Not just me, but all three of us. Come on, Dad, we can't let Mom walk into a potentially dangerous situation by herself now, can we?"

"Well, she has Susan Parker with her." Tom said weakly.

"Dad, you sound like a wimp. Mom needs you and Anne and I won't rest until we've helped to sort out this almighty mess."

"I don't have my car here, Paul. I left it in Bracebridge."

"Don't worry, we'll all go in mine. Anne, are you ready to hit the road?"

Anne had disappeared off to the washroom and had only heard the first part of the conversation. She appeared brushing her hair.

"So, what's up, bro?"

"We're going to drive to Silvercorp and help Mom talk some sense into the manager there. Are you ready?"

"You mean to say we're setting off now, right this minute? What's the rush?"

"If we leave now we'll get to the mine before closing time otherwise we will have to check into a motel or something and I don't want to be any longer than I have to. I told Atsuko that I'd be back late tonight."

"Well, it will be really, really late, Paul if we drive back tonight. Anyhow, we'll face that when we come to it, let's go then."

"What about the dogs, I can't leave them." Tom whined.

"Dad, if it makes you happy they can come with us. Come on boys, oh, but yuk, Ben still stinks."

"I'll spray him with some of my perfume, don't be such a wimp, Paul, you'll get used to the smell after a while." Anne said as she jumped into the back seat of Paul's car with Ben and Puff beside her. Taking out a small perfume bottle she proceeded to spray Ben liberally with the perfume.

"There, you smell beautiful, Benny-Boy."

"Right, off we go." Paul said as Tom climbed into the front seat and closed his door with a loud thud.

"Silvercorp here we come."

EIGHT

The drive seemed to go on and on and on and the scenery appeared to have not changed much since they had hit the Canadian Shield north of Barrie. Rose looked out of the car window at the rocky outcrops and random collection of spruce trees. It was hauntingly beautiful in a very rugged sort of way although something about the scenery set her nerves on edge. To think that the early settlers had made their way so far north and built communities which eventually became towns like New Liskeard and Timmins being the closest to Silvercorp, the mine they were heading for on their journey. Thinking about the terrain, Rose wondered where the railway line was in relation to the Highway. She knew that the railways had opened up the north long before many of the highways had been built when cars became the means of the masses, and she also knew that the railways were needed to transport valuable minerals found in the Canadian Shield such as silver, gold, cobalt, and a whole plethora of other valuable commodities needed to fuel the bourgeoning industrial revolution of the early nineteenth century. Rose thought about the Sloman's from Clinton, Fred Sloman, a teacher, his wife and five children who, along with their number of pets, travelled the northern railway lines stopping off at sidings to provide education for children living in the remote regions of Northern Ontario. There were Italian migrants working on the railways and they brought out their wives and children from Italy. Many lived in small shacks close to the lines and most of them could not speak a word of English. They welcomed the School Car on Wheels with open arms. There were also woodsmen, First Nations, lumberjacks, and fur-traders children all needing education. Some would travel for miles to attend the school often canoeing part way and walking the rest. The Sloman's taught in their little school-car-on-wheels for over thirty years.

Rose let out a deep sigh and looked at her watch. She wanted to say, "are we nearly there yet?" She stopped herself as she remembered Jessica, Anne, and Paul's plaintive little voices when they were kids asking Tom the same question whenever they went on a road trip together. Even when they were old enough to know better, she thought, recalling the trip they had taken from Ontario to British Columbia driving Jessica to her university in Vancouver, a trip that most people would take over a period of at least five days, but no, Jessica was anxious to get there and kept urging Tom to keep driving with few stops. They had reached Vancouver in three days. *That was the road trip from hell*, Rose thought as she sighed deeply again.

"Are you feeling alright?" Susan asked.

"Yes, I'm fine, just a bit tired. Maybe we could stop for a coffee and stretch our legs." Rose said hopefully.

"We're almost an hour away, Rose, and I'm really anxious to get there before the mine closes for the day. Do you mind if we just press on?"

"Of course I don't mind. Have you thought what we're going to say when we get there?"

"Yes, I've been thinking about that. Rose, could you get your phone out and look up the TSE index and see where Silvercorp stands on the stock exchange."

Rose looked at her friend with amazement. She spoke as if looking up stocks and shares was an everyday activity. Rose had never been onto the TSE in her life before, but there was always a first time for anything. She Googled the TSE and tapped in Silvercorp.

"Wow, these shares have gone sky-high in the past month. Tom's $200,000 is now worth nearly $600,000. How on earth could that be at all possible, Susan?"

"You're wrong, Rose. According to the shareholders agreement, Tom and Alex now between them own Roy and George's shares so they both have $400,000 invested which means that Tom's shares will be worth over a million dollars and now that is serious money. I do wonder, though, what's driving up the push in value. I mean, silver has always been a good investment, but never this good. Okay, we have something to talk about with the owner. That's a starting point at least."

Now that they were almost there Rose was having her extreme doubts about the wisdom of confronting the management. They would surely deny all knowledge of the 'accidental' deaths of Roy and George and the actual shareholders agreement was all above board and legal. Quite what Susan and she hoped to achieve was now sounding obscure and vague. *Oh, Tom, why did you have to get us into this mess?* Rose thought for the umpteenth time.

They could see the mine from a distance as the landscape had been scoured bare of shrubs and there was a tailing of stone and gravel everywhere. It was not a pretty sight and Rose could see why environmentalists got so upset as this was truly a case of scarring the landscape.

A big sign at the entrance to the property announced *Silvercorp is the Mine for Today.* The Porsche purred up the long driveway and came to a halt outside a single-story, concrete building, presumably the mine's headquarters. There were half a dozen cars parked in the car park, but Rose noticed another car park further down the road which was full of cars, *obviously the mine workers*, she thought as they prepared to get out of the car.

It was 4:30 p.m. The mine was due to close in one hour's time. They would have to get their skates on Rose thought as she stretched her legs and looked around her. There was a dark grey car parked out in front. Could that be the Lincoln Navigator belonging to the elusive Alex?

She was about to walk over to the car to look at the model when Susan grabbed her arm and said, "Come on, Rose, let's get this over with. Just follow my lead."

The two women walked into the airy reception room where a petite young woman sat at her computer behind the counter. She looked up as they entered and gave Susan and Rose a big, welcoming smile.

"Good afternoon, how can I help you?"

Rose looked at Susan.

"Oh, we're here to see the manager."

"Which one do you want to see, David or Brian?"

"Brian if he's available." Susan said ignoring Rose's perplexed face. It would be easier talking to someone neither of them knew, although quite who David was heaven only knew.

NINE

Paul drove like a mad man, breaking at the last minute at stop signs and overtaking when Tom would never have done so himself. Anne was oblivious to her brother's driving. She had spent most of their journey on her iPhone doing heaven only knows what, but at least she wasn't gripping the sides of the seat like Tom.

"Dad," Anne eventually said, "What's the name of that good looking detective Mom fancied? You know the one that looks like Idris Alba."

"Why do you ask," Tom said.

"Well, I'm going to get in touch with him and see if he can help. Being a detective, he would have access to a vast amount of information."

They had reached Highway 11 and could see signs for New Liskeard and Haileybury. The mine was located somewhere between Timmins and New Liskeard. Tom vaguely recalled something about the Porcupine Gold Rush which was also situated up near Timmins where they had mined over five times the amount of gold ever retrieved from the whole of the Klondike Gold Rush. There was also the Cobalt Silver Rush which had started in 1903 when the Temiskaming and the Northern Ontario railway lines were being built. One of the railway workers had accidently discovered a huge vein of silver, and within a decade the Cobalt Silver Rush had produced nine percent of the world's silver, producing 460 million ounces of the ore. *Quite remarkable,* Tom thought as he looked out at the rather desolate scenery before him.

They could see the mine from miles away as it certainly was a scar on the landscape. Piles of rock and gravel spanned the scrubland around the mine rather like a quarry. Tom thought about how the jungles of the Congo in Africa had been decimated by miners clearing great swaths of trees killing off the natural habitat and destroying the fragile balance of nature. *Man has a lot to answer for,* he thought as they neared the entrance to the mine. Paul pulled over to the side of the road before entering the driveway to the mine.

"So, Dad, what's the plan?"

"Could I use your phone love, and I'll see if I can get hold of your mother. I suspect that they're already here ahead of us." He looked at his watch. It was already five o'clock and the mine would be closing in half an hour's time.

"You can't just go blustering in accusing them of murdering your friends, can you?" Anne chirped up from behind Tom in the back seat of Paul's car.

This is rich, Tom thought, Paul and Anne had practically dragged him there and now they were unsure of their actions.

She tapped in Rose's telephone number from behind Tom in the back seat of Paul's car and handed the phone to her father. There was no answer and eventually he was directed to voicemail.

"Well, that was a fat load of good," Tom said, "I suppose now that we're here we should at least go and introduce ourselves."

Paul eased back on to the road and drove up the driveway and parked his car by the not so impressive office building. All three of them got out of the car and stretched their legs. Tom immediately noticed the dark grey Lincoln Navigator parked three cars down from what could only be Susan Parker's silver Porsche which Paul was now eyeing intently.

"That's Susan Parker's car," Tom said as he walked past it to the Lincoln.

"This car here I swear is Alex Boychuk's car, you know, the one that almost ran me over in Bayfield and was tracking me in Bracebridge."

Paul joined his dad as he peered through the windows.

"Nice wheels. Oh, no, Dad, look, I think there's blood over here on the tailgate."

Tom rushed over to where Paul was standing and peeped through the back window. Inside all he could see was a plaid blanket but outside, on the tailgate, there were definite drops of blood.

"I'm going to check in the back," Tom said as he opened the rear door. Sure enough, when he opened the rear tailgate his senses were hit by a strong metallic smell. Lifting the corner of the plaid blanket there, before their eyes, was a mass of congealed blood.

"Oh, yuk. Dad, I think that I'm going to be sick." Paul heaved and then violently bought up his lunch.

Tom had opened the back door and was regarding the

copious amounts of blood objectively. There was no sign of a body anywhere.

Anne who had been admiring Susan's Porsche started to walk towards the men.

"Stay there, love, this is not a pretty sight. In fact, can you phone 911 and get the police here. Come on, Paul, let's go and speak to the management."

TEN

Susan and Rose waited until the receptionist called them into the manager's office. They walked into a light, modern room. There was a man standing by the window with his back to the door. There was something about him that looked familiar, but Rose couldn't quite put her finger on it until he turned around and to her astonishment she realized that she was looking at none other than Brian Henderson the current Bayfield Croquet Club President. The shock of seeing Brian standing there had rendered Rose speechless, but Susan Parker was totally unaware of any of this. She stepped forward and stretched out her hand to be shaken. Brian took Susan's hand, smiled his most disarming smile and then looked Rose straight in the eye.

"Delighted to see you again, Rose. Is Tom with you?"

Susan looked shocked, "So, you know each other?"

"Yes, Brian is our Croquet Club President. We've known each other for almost twenty years."

Brian and his wife, Sylvia, had moved to the village almost the same time that Tom and Rose had settled into their charming house on Bayfield Terrace. They never met each other until both couples had joined the croquet club and, as beginners, took the same classes together. Sylvia and Rose had hit it off right away and had become good friends having coffee and lunch together, even forming a book club. They had been great friends until Sylvia took a part-time job working for the County Planner in Goderich and that curtailed their coffee mornings. Rose still met Sylvia for the occasional lunch, but life had got in the way of their friendship and, although when the two of them did manage to meet everything was as before, Rose had sensed a pulling-away of their friendship. As to Brian, well, he played the odd game of golf with Tom and since being the President of the Croquet Club they had not seen much of him at all.

"So, what are you doing here, Brian?" Rose said having recovered from her initial surprise.

"Well, I own the mine, my dear. Admittedly in theory I've retired, but I still keep my hand in and come up here once or twice a month. But more to the point, what are you two delightful women doing here?"

Rose looked at Susan as she was supposed to be taking the lead.

"Well, we've come to talk about the Bayfield consortium headed up by Alex Boychuk. You know, I presume, about the deaths of George and Roy, two out of the four shareholders..."

Brian interrupted Susan mid-flow, looking at his watch he said, "Would you two like me to show you around the mine before it closes up for the day. Look, if we go now we could just about do the tour before the men all lock up and leave. We can talk as we walk, right?"

Susan and Rose didn't have time to answer as Brian was up and walking out of his office as he spoke. They ran after him passing the young receptionist who called out bye to them as they left the building. They followed Brian to an open tunnel.

"This here is the entrance to the mine which, by the way, was an existing silver mine first mined during the Porcupine Gold Rush in the early nineteenth century. It was closed in 1970 and remained so until 1995 when I bought it and the rest is history. We've gone from strength to strength discovering new seams and veins of silver as we go."

Susan interrupted him, "Yes, we noticed on the stock exchange Silvercorp has gone up over three times in the past six months. Why would that be? It seems somewhat extreme particularly as in the world of commodities silver generally is not as valuable as gold or platinum."

Brian stopped mid-stride causing Rose to almost walk into the back of him. He turned and gave the two women a strange look.

"So, you've been doing a bit of research then. Well, I'm going to let you into a little secret one that the general public is not yet aware and that is that we have discovered lithium and traces of tantalum beneath the seams of silver. Now both those minerals are a rare commodity, they are used in cellphones and until recently ninety percent of those minerals have come from mines in the Congo, but that country is politically unstable. If we can mine them here then we sure are on to a winner."

Brian had reached an elevator which looked rather like a metal cage. He opened the door and ushered Rose and Susan inside.

"Right, we're going to descend three hundred feet down into the main mine shaft. Here, put these helmets on and hold tight as we go down."

Rose and Susan put on the hard hats and stepped into the elevator. Their meeting with the Silvercorp manager certainly had not gone as they had planned, but it would be interesting visiting the actual mine as neither of them had ever been down a mine shaft before. It was with great trepidation as they descended into the bowels of the earth. The elevator bumped to a sudden halt and Brian stepped out and beckoned to the women to follow. They were in a very large cavern with re-enforced sides, the sound of machinery drilling making talking quite difficult. Brian pointed to three huge metal containers filled with rocks. He picked one up and pointed to a vein of shiny looking metal.

"This is what raw silver looks like, not very impressive is it?"

He was right, the thin line of shiny metal did not look particularly exciting, but then Brian took out a small hammer and placing the rock on the floor he cracked it open. Inside what looked like a line of silver immediately appeared all over the surface area of the cracked stone.

"Wow, that's amazing," Rose said, "You mean to say all of these rocks are the same?"

Brian nodded. "Right, let me show you the processing room." He led the two women to a door in the corner of the large cavern. He opened it and ushered Susan and Rose inside. Before they could say a word, Brian had backed out and slammed the door behind him. He then went back to the elevator, got in and proceeded to ascend back up to the surface and mine entrance. He would deal with the pesky women later when the mine was closed and there would be nobody around to witness anything.

ELEVEN

Tom and Paul entered the office building and immediately were greeted by the receptionist who pointedly looked at the clock hanging on the wall opposite her desk. It was five twenty and the office and mine were due to close in ten minutes.

"Oh, how can I help you?"

"We're looking for the manager and it's pretty urgent." Tom said glancing around the room as if the manager would appear, like magic from nowhere.

"Umm... he's not here at the moment but he'll be back pretty soon as the office closes in ten minutes. You could take a seat and wait for him if you like."

Paul and Tom sat down and then Tom jumped up again.

"Have two women been here?"

"Yes, just twenty minutes ago. Brian took them on a quick tour of the mine. That's where he is right now."

Paul was now on his feet looking out of the window.

"Come on, Dad, let's get going." Paul practically dragged his father out of the office.

"Dad, he's taken them into the mine. Come on, we have to go and find them as they could be in danger."

Tom ran after Paul towards the main entrance to the mine. Just as they reached the tunnel a loud horn blasted the air making the men jump with surprise. Footsteps clattering and voices getting louder and louder could be heard coming from the tunnel. Suddenly they were surrounded by men wearing hard hat's, all looking sweaty and grimy, over a hundred men walked out of the tunnel and went over to the ticket puncher near the office. They had to clock in and clock out just as miners and factory workers had done throughout the centuries.

Tom and Paul felt as if they were fighting a losing battle against the tide of humanity trying to get inside the mine whilst all the miners were coming out in the opposite direction. There was no point in trying to move forward, they would just have to wait until the wave of men had subsided.

Brian was also on his way out and back to the office when he saw Tom and Paul. He quickly walked back inside the tunnel convinced that he had not been seen. There were several ways out of the mine; he would take another route and double back to the office. It appeared now that dealing with Alex, a.k.a David, was to be only part of his troubles. Tom would have to be dealt with, as would his nosey wife and friend.

TWELVE

Susan and Rose were momentarily dazed when the door shut behind them. It had been so unexpected and sudden. They had been plunged into darkness until Susan flipped her phone flashlight on. She took her helmet off and began to fiddle with the built in lamp on top of the hat.

"Bingo," she cried as a bright light flared into life. "Here you go, Rose, just flick this switch here."

As Rose's helmet light also flared up they looked around the small room that they had been locked in and realized that it most certainly was not a processing room, more like a store room of sorts. There were shelves with great coils of wire stacked on top of boxes of who knew what. There were brooms and buckets and even a commercial vacuum cleaner in the corner of the room.

"I don't suppose it's worth shouting for help, is it?" Rose said in a small voice, "and I know without saying that our cell-phones won't work down here, so, I guess we'll have to try to get this door opened somehow."

Susan was studying the door handle carefully.

"There's no keyhole so I can't pick the lock although I might be able to loosen the jam. Do you have anything metal that I could use in your purse, Rose?"

Susan had left her own purse in the Porsche, but Rose always carried a small shoulder bag which contained her wallet, keys, a lipstick, and, joy of joys, some tweezers. She handed them over to Susan.

"There you go, don't worry if you break them."

Susan pulled the tweezers open so that she could use just one sharp end to work the lock.

"You might as well sit down for a while Rose as this is going to take a lot of time and patience."

Rose upturned one of the buckets and sat down to watch her friend at work.

Back in the car park, Anne waited patiently for the police to arrive. She had taken the dogs out of the car and walked them around the car park and was just trying to coax them back inside the car when a pretty, young woman emerged from the office building and looked at her quizzically.

"Are you waiting for someone?" she asked Anne.

"Yes, the police. There's a huge amount of blood in the back of that car over there." Anne pointed to the Lincoln. "Do you know the owner of the vehicle?"

The young woman had turned quite pale. She looked from Anne to the car and back again.

"Yes, that's David's car. Are you sure that it's human blood as we do get a lot of deer out here? Oh my God, you don't think that it's David's blood, do you? He was quite alive at lunch time today, in fact Brian and he went into Timmins for a bite to eat."

The police cars could be heard long before they arrived on the scene. The miners had all gone by then, only a few stragglers were left.

"You had better stay," Anne said as she could see the indecision in the receptionist's face. "The police, I am sure, will want to interview you. You may well have been the last person to have seen Alex, umm...I mean, David alive."

The young woman shuddered and walked over to where Anne was standing.

"Lovely dogs, what are their names?"

"Oh, this is Ben and this is Puff. Do you know where my dad and brother got to?" she asked the receptionist, "and for that matter, my mother and her friend, where did they all go?"

"Now, that I can answer you as Mr. Henderson, the manager, took them on a tour of the mine about forty minutes ago. They should be back by now."

The police pulled up in front of the building and four policemen jumped out. Anne introduced herself and showed them the way to the Lincoln Navigator.

"This young woman said that Alex, umm... I mean David, owns the vehicle." Anne turned to the receptionist and said. "I'm so sorry I didn't get your name?"

"Sandy," she said, "Pleased to meet you."

"I'm Anne and my dad and brother are the two men that came into your office half an hour ago. Do you know where they are?"

"Yes, the minute that I told them that the two women were being given a tour of the mine they left in a big hurry. They are probably down the mine shaft by now."

Anne got hold of one of the policemen. "Quick, my family

might be in danger, they're inside the mine. Please can you help me find them."

Two burly policemen followed Anne towards the tunnel. Just then another car turned up and parked next to Susan's Porsche. A tall, handsome, black man stepped out, followed by a blond headed lean looking man. DCI Hargreaves and DI Trevor Manning had arrived.

THIRTEEN

"Bingo," Susan shouted after hearing the lock click. She turned the handle and the door opened.

"Oh, gosh, you're a genius." Rose said jumping up and down, "A real genius. We're free, let's go."

They both headed out of the storeroom and into the large cavern. Both women had heard the loud foghorn announcing the end of the working day for the miners. That had been ten minutes ago and now there was an eerie silence. Suddenly the mechanical sound of the cage-like elevator shattered the silence and Rose and Susan immediately watched as the elevator descended into the cavern. To their amazement and utter joy, Tom and Paul stepped out.

"Tom, Paul," Rose called out as she ran to greet them. "How did you find us?" She clung on to Tom as if her life depended on it. Susan just smiled and said, "So you decided to check out the mine too? Did you meet the owner, Brian Henderson?"

Tom stopped in his tracks. "You don't mean Brian Henderson from Bayfield? What on earth has he got to do with Silvercorp?"

Rose interrupted Tom, "He bought the mine twenty years ago Tom, and although he's retired he still comes up twice a month for business meetings. I don't think that your friend, Alex, is really called that, I think that he's Brian's partner, David Grantham, although I'm not one hundred percent sure. All I know is that Brian has a partner called David. Isn't that right, Susan?"

Susan had stepped into the elevator and was anxious to get out of the mine. What she hadn't told Rose was that she suffered from claustrophobia and being hundreds of feet down in the bowels of the earth had made her feel distinctly queasy.

Tom and Paul led Rose into the elevator while Tom told Rose about the Lincoln Navigator and the copious amounts of blood found in the back of the vehicle.

"You see love, that's Alex's car. I'm convinced something bad has happened to him. Anne called the police. They're probably in the car park right now. As to that Brian, heaven knows what he's got up to."

Brian had decided to play it cool. He walked over to the car park where Anne, Sandy, and two men were standing talking. He noticed three police cars and yellow tape draped around David's car.

"What's going on here?" he said to Sandy who was looking very agitated and kept looking at her watch. He knew that she had a young family waiting for her at home and she was already half an hour later leaving work than normal.

"Oh, Mr. Henderson, the police have found loads of blood

in Mr. Grantham's car. They think something might have happened to him."

Officer Manning stepped forward. "Are you the owner of the mine, sir?"

Brian puffed himself up and answered rather haughtily. "Yes, my partner is David Grantham and I believe that's his car you're inspecting. What's with all the yellow tape?"

DCI Hargreaves joined the men but remained silent as he observed the owner of the mine. Brian was an imposing man and obviously, by the tone of his voice, someone used to being obeyed. He had to be in his sixties, greying hair with a strong chin, and lean body. DCI Hargreaves listened as Officer Manning fired off questions.

"We believe that Mr. Grantham had lunch with you today, your receptionist said that you both left the office together around noon. That was the last she saw of Mr. Grantham. Tell me about your lunch."

"David and I drove together in his car to Timmins, about a fifteen-minute journey. We had lunch at Crabby Joes, talked mostly business and then drove back to the office around one thirty. I left him sitting in his car making some phone calls. I returned to my office where I stayed all afternoon until I was interrupted by two women. I gave them a quick tour of the mine and that's all."

DCI Hargreaves thought that Brian Henderson was a cool customer as he was far too smooth and appeared to have a ready explanation at hand for everything. What Brian didn't know, however, was that after John had received the rather panicked phone call from Rose's daughter Anne, who had said that her mother and Susan were in danger and were at the Silvercorp mine near Timmins. After that call he had pulled out all stops to

research not only the mine, but Brian Henderson and his partner, David Grantham. He had dug deep and had found very
little to red-flag the company or the owners, until he had entered
the one word, 'consortium' into the search engine. It was here
that he noticed a pattern emerging. Over the past two years, four
consortiums had ended up passing up their shares to one single
share holder. There were four different names as single shareholders. John had entered these names into his search engine, no
red-flags, but all four names had addresses in Huron County. He
checked out the addresses and soon found that the names did not
correlate with the addresses. He did a driver's license check and,
once again found that there were no drivers registered under the
names. It was beginning to look like all four consortium leaders
used false names or, more feasibly, it was the same man using
different alias'. Was David Grantham or, for that matter, Brian
Henderson, using pseudonyms to set up the consortiums?

Just as these thoughts were whirling around his mind, John
spotted Rose, Tom, Susan, and Paul coming out of the
entrance to the mine. The last time that he had seen Rose had
been at Christmas when Kate, Rose's sister and he had joined
the Blair's for Christmas lunch. Anne and the children had
been there too and Paul, Atsuko, and their young family. It had
been noisy and lovely and, maybe it was just as well as he had
had no time with Rose by herself. Indeed, they had both been
studiously avoiding each other and that was the way it had to
be; Kate was the woman he loved and wanted to spend the rest
of his life with, Rose was just a distraction.

Rose stopped in full stride when she saw John Hargreaves
standing next to another police officer. Susan reacted first.

"Oh, look, it's Trevor. He must have responded to Anne's

911 call. That's great, I haven't seen him in years, but look Rose, isn't that DCI Hargreaves? What on earth is he doing here?"

"Yes, and how did he get here so quickly from London?" Tom said remembering Anne's conversation in the car. He had known that she had texted John but quite what she had said was beyond him.

"Look, Rose," Susan said pointing to Brian, "There's that slime ball of a toad, what was his name, umm... Brian, yes, Brian Henderson."

Brian was marching towards them arms outstretched and in a booming voice so all could hear he said, "So there you two are? I was about to send out a search party. What happened? One minute you were there in front of me, and the next, you had disappeared."

Rose and Susan looked at him incredulously.

"You know that you locked us in the storeroom, you liar." They both shouted together.

"Of course I did no such thing, how very ridiculous."

Officer Manning intervened, but not before smiling at Susan and mouthing a silent greeting.

"Now, if you don't mind, sir, we have some further questions to ask you. Is there somewhere we can go where we can talk in private?"

"Yes, my office would be fine, but I do have to say that I had hoped to be out of here by now. I promised my wife that I would get the 8:00 p.m. flight from Timmins to London."

"Right, well follow me and let's get it done. Are you going to join us, DCI Hargreaves?"

John, who had been talking to Tom and Rose, turned and

said, "I'll be there shortly, start the interview without me. I need to talk to the Blairs first."

"Now, where were we? Yes, I was telling you about the different consortiums found under different names not one of which checked out. Tomorrow I'm going to visit some of the actual shareholders and show them a photo of our Alex, or should I say, David and see if what I suspect is the case that he had repeated the whole shareholder scam multiple times."

"But John," Rose interrupted, "the shareholder agreement is all above board and legally binding. I didn't think that Silvercorp would be liable for any legal action against them unless it could be proved that the accidental deaths were not actual accidents. I'm afraid we've already been down that road."

"Yes, you may be right on that count, but it looks like we might have a murder on our hands here. Judging by the amount of blood in the back of the car I suspect our Alex is no longer with us. Our challenge now is to find the body."

"Are forensics on to it?" Susan said while looking over her shoulder at the taped off area around the Lincoln.

"Yes, officer Manning, who, by the way, Susan, remembers you fondly, anyway, he strikes me as being very efficient, he's got the SOC and forensics here working as I speak."

"So, what will you do now, John?" Rose asked tentatively. She was still finding his close proximity awkward. *Damn,* she thought, *the chemistry is still there.*

John stared at Rose and for a second his breath was taken away. How was it that she managed to disturb his very equilibrium?

"When we've finished interviewing Brian Henderson I would like to drive around this mine area and look for tyre tracks that might match the Lincoln Navigator's. We need a body before we can build our case."

Just then they were interrupted by Anne and Sandy and two panting dogs. Ben and Puff were pulling the women along at a fast pace. Just who was taking whom for a walk was anyone's guess. As the dogs approached Tom and Rose, they jumped up with unbridled pleasure at seeing their owners again. Rose threw her arms around Ben and then Puff in an affectionate hug.

"Oh, I've missed you two darlings."

Tom looked at his watch and then turned to John who was about to walk into the office to join officer Manning.

"John, you don't need us here anymore, do you? I think that we're going to head back to the Muskokas now and get an early start tomorrow morning for Bayfield."

"Yes," Rose said, "we've got some Airbnb guests checking in to Kate's cottage in the afternoon so we will have to leave really early."

"And I have to get back to Toronto. I promised Alan that I'd pick the kids up tomorrow evening." Anne chirped in.

"Come on dogs," Rose said, "Let's get back in the car. Oh, Susan, do you want me to travel with you?"

Susan smiled and said, "No, I think that I'll check into a motel in Timmins as I'd like to catch up with Trevor. It's almost thirty years since we last saw each other and there's been a lot of water under the bridge since then. Do you know, John, if he's married or not?"

John laughed and said that Trevor had revealed that he had just gone through a mucky divorce.

"Okay, then that's sealed it, I'll see you back in Bayfield Rose- maybe not tomorrow, but certainly the next day."

The two friends hugged each other and waved as Tom, Paul, Rose, and Anne, not forgetting the dogs, all piled into Paul's little car.

Rather them than me. Susan thought as she got into her silver Porsche preparing to wait for Trevor Manning to rap up his interview.

FOURTEEN

Officer Manning and DCI Hargreaves sat in two chairs facing Brian Henderson. They had deliberately arranged the chairs so that Brian wasn't sitting behind his desk in his 'owner of the mine' status. The man was already too confident for their liking; he needed to be brought down a peg or two. Unfortunately, the officers had no recording devise with them, although John laid his phone down on the table between them and pressed the recording button. It would have to do, as would the standard Miranda rights about to be read to Brian Henderson.

"Please note that you do not have to say anything, but anything you may say will be recorded and used in a court of law and may not be beneficial to your defence."

Brian looked incredulous.

"You've got to be kidding. Are you actually arresting me? May I ask what for?"

"Of course we're not arresting you we're following standard police procedure that's all. We could take you down to the police station if you would prefer and then we could detain you overnight. Maybe we should do just that."

Brian's bluster left him and he looked immediately deflated like all the air had been sucked out of a balloon.

"Oh, no, I do apologize and I'm appreciative of your consideration by interviewing me here and not at the police station. Can we start again, now how can I help you officers?"

Trevor took the lead.

"When was the last time that you saw David Grantham?"

"We both had lunch together at Crabbie Joes in Timmins. David drove and I went with him. We left the restaurant at around 1:10 p.m. and got back here at 1:30. I remember that because I had a tele-conference call booked for 1:30 and I rushed into my office just in time. Sandy will verify all of this."

"Sandy. Who is Sandy?" Trevor asked although he had a fair idea that she was the receptionist.

"Sandy is our receptionist, great gal, she'll be able to fill you in with details like David's meeting schedules etc. She's out in the car park if you wanted to talk to her."

"Yes, we'll have a word with her after we're done here. Right, John, you had some questions you wanted to ask, didn't you?"

John cleared his throat and with his educated English accent began, "So, Mr Henderson, tell me about the consortiums that David Grantham set up using pseudonyms."

Brian was clearly rattled, but he managed to keep his cool.

"I'm not sure what you are talking about? Pseudonyms, that's totally bizarre, I do know that at least four consortiums were formed and as far as I know the shareholders have done very well out of it. David and I did discuss the shareholders agreements and terms, oh, that was over two years ago now. I remember getting our legal team on to it. You do know that our shares have hit the roof."

"And why is that Mr. Henderson?" John asked smoothly as he watched Brian's face torn between telling the truth or fabricating some lie.

"Okay, I'll tell you, but this is not yet public knowledge as I'm still waiting on legal advice on all of this. So, when I bought the mine it had been closed for over thirty years, apparently depleted of all silver. I studied geology at university, so I know a thing or two about minerals and I also know that the Canadian Shield knows no bounds for ores trapped within the granite rock. It all boils down to extraction you see and thirty years ago they did not have lasers and computerized sophisticated machinery that we have today. In a nutshell we discovered large seams of silver, but the deeper we mined we discovered another ore embedded in the rock, lithium and traces of tantalum. These are both quite rare commodities used mostly in cell phones and are worth a heck of a lot more than silver, hence the rise in the stock market. You see, at the moment silver and lithium had been lumped together so the shareholders are unaware that it's the lithium that is driving the massive increase. We are happy to float the two separately, but as I said before, our legal teams are still working out all the protocols and procedures."

John could see that Trevor was anxious to get back to the case of the blood in David Grantham's car. He looked at Trevor and nodded to him.

"So, you last saw David sitting in his car. What was he doing? Why didn't he follow you into the office?"

"Well, I can't answer that officer, can I? I mean I knew that my teleconference call was at 1:30 and so I rushed inside just in time to take the call which, incidentally, lasted over an hour. I then got on with a huge backlog of paperwork and was thoroughly immersed in that right up until I was interrupted by Rose Blair and her friend. I'm sure that Sandy can vouch for that."

Trevor nodded and then asked whether David was an asset to the mine and Silvercorp in general.

"To be honest most of the time David has been left running the show on his own. I come up here twice a month, sometimes I spend a couple of days, other times longer. At the moment everything is running pretty smoothly and I suppose I have to thank David for that."

"You say that rather begrudgingly." John said.

"No, I don't begrudge David at all. He's hard working and seems to have loads of energy. Mind you, he's a good ten years younger than me too."

"So, in your opinion, what do you think has happened to David?"

There was a pause while Brian thought. "To be honest I haven't got a clue as to where he's gone. You're the detectives, I'll leave that mystery for you to solve. Now, if you don't mind, I really will have to go. My plane leaves in forty minutes and it's a ten-minute drive to the airport. I'll give you my business card with all my contact details. If you need to reach me feel free to do so any time."

It was clear that the interview was over and that they would not get anything further from him. Brian stood up and extended his hand to shake. Showing the men the door, he quickly grabbed his briefcase and followed the two detectives, and locked the door as he left.

Sandy was sitting outside waiting patiently to be interviewed herself. She had watched the forensic team as they dusted the Lincoln Navigator for prints and took samples of fibre and, of course samples of the blood. She was impressed with the speed and efficiency of the team. The police were often maligned but seeing them in action now made her realize how lucky they were to have a good, reliable police force, particularly where they lived up in northern Ontario, the boonies, as some people might say.

She was approached by the blond-haired officer.

"Sandy, is it? Could I have a quick word with you, and I promise it will be quick, but you might have to come to the police station tomorrow to make a full statement if that would be okay?"

Sandy looked at her watch and let out a gasp. She was already almost an hour late for picking the kids up from daycare.

"If you promise to make it quick, I have to pick my kids up."

"Right, we need to just verify a few things. When was the last time that you saw David Grantham?"

"It was lunch time. Mr. Henderson and he were heading out for lunch together and that was around 12:00 p.m."

"And when did they get back from lunch?"

"Well, I didn't see Mr. Grantham return to his office, but Mr. Henderson rushed in at about 1:30 just as the telephone started to ring. He had a conference call booked for 1:30."

"And you say that you didn't see Mr. Grantham again?"

"No, he didn't return to the office, but that's not at all unusual. He often would go to meetings and I'd not see him until the next day. There was really nothing unusual about today."

"Okay, you may go now. If you do think of anything significant that you need to tell us, I'll give you my card and don't hesitate to call me. Oh, and pop into the station tomorrow to make a formal statement."

Sandy smiled and grabbing her purse, she quickly jumped into her car and drove off at a speed which made Trevor raise his eyebrows.

"Time to call it a day, John." he said and then he spotted Susan Parker getting out of her sleek, silver Porsche.

"Hi there, Trevor. What are you doing tonight? Do you fancy joining me for dinner, we could catch up on the past thirty years over a bottle of wine?"

She was a cracker of a woman, Trevor thought, quite stunning. How could he resist such a blast from the past. With a broad smile across his handsome face he said, "I would love to have dinner with you. Where did you have in mind?"

"Aha, now I leave that for you to decide as this is your stomping ground. I've just booked into the Golden Goose Motel on Carriage Lane so maybe a restaurant somewhere in that vicinity?"

"Right, why don't you go and check in and I'll pick you up around 7:30 p.m."

Susan smiled. She liked a decisive man, and she had such a good feeling about Trevor.

"Okay, see you later."

FIFTEEN

John had listened to their conversation and had to quietly suppress a laugh. Susan Parker was unstoppable, but she was a lovely woman and he wished her well. Thinking of lovely women, he thought of Rose and then immediately felt racked with guilt. Kate should have come to mind, not her sister. He shook his head and let out a loud sigh. A drive around the area surrounding the mine would help clear his head and then it would be straight to the airport to catch his plane. It occurred to John that he, in all likelihood, would be on the same plane as Brian Henderson. He did not feel like company so he would lay low and keep out of Brian's way.

Driving through the Silvercorp mine area John was reminded of a moonscape. Tall, slag heaps raised up like small mountains surrounded toxic looking tailing ponds. Desolate was the word that came to mind, however, looking at the foreboding water of the tailing ponds John was acutely aware that a body could easily disappear into the murky depths and never be seen again. He would suggest that a dredger be used by the police as the water would be too toxic and soupy for a diving team.

Arriving at the airport with barely twenty minutes to spare before take-off, John immediately saw Brian Henderson. He was sitting next to a strikingly beautiful woman. Before John could find a seat for himself in the small departures lounge, Brian had waved him over.

"I thought that we would end up on the same flight. Maddie, this is DCI Henderson."

John extended his hand to shake hers.

"Pleased to meet you, umm... Maddie."

Brian could see John's hesitation. He laughingly cried out, "You think that she's my bit on the side, don't you? Maddie is my stepdaughter. She was up visiting her grandparents. They're both in a retirement home in Timmins. Actually, David Grantham is her uncle, my wife's brother-in-law."

This was getting rather complicated, John thought as he sat down and made a mental note of what he had just learnt. So, Brian Henderson's wife had been married before and had a child by that marriage? Her brother was the connecting link.

"Was it David who brought you into the mine take-over or the other way around?"

"Well, it was a bit of both really as you see, I met my wife Sylvia on my first visit to Silvercorp way back in the early nineties. Her brother-in-law had worked at the mine years before it closed so he had a good working knowledge. Sylvia also used to work as a receptionist before the mine closed. When I met her, she was working here at the airport and Maddie was just a wee chubby five-year-old." Brian winked at her and she playfully slapped him, "Dad, stop calling me chubby."

She was far from chubby, John thought, indeed her long, slender legs were perfect. She was older than John would have guessed. If Brian had owned the mine for thirty years and she had been five when he first met her then that put her around thirty-five, not the twenty-something that he had first estimated.

Right then the passengers were called to board the plane to London.

SIXTEEN

Rose, Tom, and the dogs arrived back in Bayfield at 1:00 p.m. exactly one hour before the Airbnb guests were due to check-in at 2:00 p.m. Paul and Anne had driven their parents into Bracebridge so that Tom could retrieve his car and then they had headed off to London leaving their mom and dad to make their own way back to the cottage and then back to Bayfield. It was at times like this that Rose regretted having agreed to look after her sister's cottage. Under normal circumstances they would have enjoyed a leisurely drive back home, instead it was a mad dash to reach the village before the 2:00 p.m. check-in.

"Thank goodness I'd prepared the cottage before we left," Rose said to Tom who was busy ushering the dogs into their back garden.

"Yes, love, that was good thinking on your part. Would you like a cup of tea?"

"Oh, I'd love one and there are some scones which need eating that we can have with our tea."

Scones were not Rose's favourite thing even though she seemed to be forever baking them. She preferred a good muffin or bagel if given the choice.

Rose looked at the calendar pinned to their pantry door. Tomorrow was the Croquet Club cocktail party and it was being hosted by none other than the President, Brian Henderson. Thinking of the man himself Rose fairly bristled at the blatant lie that he had told everyone at the mine. She wasn't quite sure how she would face him at the cocktail party. Just then her phone rang. It was Rose's sister Kate.

"Hi, Rose," she shouted down the phone. Kate had such a loud voice and was unaware that she sounded as if she was shouting down the phone.

"Hi, Kate, we've just got in and after a cup of tea I'm going to go over to your place to meet your guests at two. How are things with you?"

"Oh, everything's great. John said that he saw you up at the mine near Timmins. What on earth were you doing there?"

At the mention of John, Rose felt her heart constrict a little. When would she stop feeling this way, she thought as she answered her sister.

"Oh, it's an awfully long story, I'll tell you next time we get together, suffice to say Susan and I had our own little adventure. When are you coming to visit us?"

It had been almost a month since Kate had driven to Bayfield and had lunch with Tom and Rose. If truth be known Rose missed having her sister living just around the corner, but she was happy for her as London seemed to be the right place for her and of course John.

"Actually, that was one of the reasons why I called. It's

John's birthday coming up and I'm going to throw him a surprise party next Friday. Can you and Tom come?"

Rose thought quickly. They were meeting Jessica and the girls in Kingston on the Wednesday spending the night and then coming back on the Thursday.

"We can come but we'll have Ella and Abby with us as they're staying for the week. Would that be okay?"

"That would be great. Okay, I must dash. I'll give you a call in a few days time when I've finalized the details. Give my love to Tom."

No sooner had Rose put the phone down when it rang again. She grabbed it and rather impatiently answered, "Rose speaking."

It was John Hargreaves.

"Are you alright, Rose? You sound rattled."

Rose took a deep breath and said, "Oh, I'm just fine. How can I help you, John?"

"I've been doing some digging on the 'deep-net' and found four consortiums for Silvercorp headed up by four different people who I believe are all the same person but under different alias like our Alex Boychuk who is really David Grantham. I've also been following a line of research into Brian Henderson. Do you know his wife, Sylvia?"

"Yes, I know her quite well. We used to see quite a lot of each other before she got a job working for the County Planner. Why do you ask?"

"Well, it transpires that Sylvia was married to Michael Grantham, David Grantham's brother. Does that ring any bells for you?"

Michael Grantham, the name did sound familiar, Rose

thought, but where had she recognized the name from somewhere in her distant past?"

"Sorry, John, I can't remember, but the name definitely sounds familiar. Funny, though, Sylvia never mentioned that she had been married before."

"Yes, well, I met her daughter, Maddie last night at the airport. I did a bit of a Google search on Sylvia's first husband, Michael. He was a lecturer at Queen's University way back in the 1970s. Apparently there was a big scandal; it transpires that he was having relationships with some of his students. He ended up taking his own life in 1973.

Rose vaguely recalled something of the scandal although she had met Tom by then and was only focused on their relationship and nothing or nobody else.

"Poor Sylvia," Rose said, "and you said that she had a daughter. How old was she when her dad died?"

"She was about five. Her mom left Kingston and got a job working as a receptionist at Silvercorp. I'm sure that her brother-in-law David helped her. Anyway, she moved back to Timmins where her parents lived. She didn't meet Brian until the early nineties when he bought the mine. They married a year later."

Rose interrupted John, "You don't think that Sylvia has anything to do with what's going on at the mine, do you?"

"I'm not sure what to think yet, Rose, but I have one request of you. Do you know the two widows, Roy and George's wives? If you do, then can you ask them if they attended university and if so when?"

"Well, that's easy. I can tell you right now that they both went to Queen's just as I did."

"Great, right, that's all I wanted to know so I must be

getting on. It was lovely seeing you again, Rose. Take care of yourself."

Before Rose could answer, John had clicked off and she was left holding the telephone in her hand and nursing a broken heart.

SEVENTEEN

Susan drove back to Bayfield at a breakneck speed, weaving in and of traffic, overtaking large transporter trucks and lumber trailers, doing speeds of over 150 mph. All the while she was recalling her evening spent with Trevor the previous night. It had been one long reminiscing, catching up on thirty years worth of both their careers. Because Trevor had always wanted to stay in Timmins, his rise up the ranks and career ladder appeared much less exacting than Susan's. He was Superintendent of the OPP office in Timmins and had his fair share of murder cases, but most of his work was either drug related or domestic abuse. Susan had veered the conversation away from her own meteoric rise by asking about Silvercorp, particularly David Grantham. She was surprised when Trevor had pulled a long face and told her that David had been red-flagged years ago, in fact, even as a young man, David had walked a fine line between what was legal and what was breaking the law. His latest venture had been the proposed casino. Rumour had it that he had joined up with some unsavoury loan-sharks and that he was in over his head. As to the consortiums, yes, Trevor had also heard about them but as far as he knew they were all legal and above board. The other interesting piece of information Susan had gleaned from talking to Trevor was that Brian's wife, Sylvia was in fact David Grantham's ex sister-in-law. Her first husband, Michael Grantham had been a professor at Queens University, but had taken his own life after a scandal at the school involving some of the students. There was much to tell Rose, Susan thought and hopefully over a glass of wine or two, she would also tell Rose how the latter part of the evening with Trevor had worked out.

Tom had gone to meet the Airbnb guests before heading over to Goderich for a doctor's appointment. He looked at his watch and thought that he would still have time to go for a quick sail before dinner that night, providing he didn't have to wait too long for his appointment. One hour later Tom was pacing up and down the waiting room already half an hour over his appointed time. The trouble was that he did need to have this check-up as two years ago he had a heart attack and his old clicker now needed to be monitored closely. He had been lucky and the medical team had been great, but his recovery had been slow and in many ways, more trying than the actual heart attack itself. For a start, the doctors had insisted that he shed some weight. Rose had been pretty strict about his diet and over a period of six months he had managed to lose over thirty-pounds which had indeed, reduced his blood-pressure and, if truth be known, made him feel ten years younger. However, the worse part of his recovery had been his overall anxiety and depression which could not easily be explained other than the fact that it was a common enough symptom of heart attack survivors. Now nearly two years later, the cloud over his head had finally lifted. He was still more anxious than he used to be, but the depression had been replaced with something even worse: memory loss. Tom's biggest concern was not for his heart, but his mind. He was convinced that he had the beginnings of dementia and that really, really scared him.

Finally, he was called in to see his doctor and by the end of the check-up he was declared to be in excellent shape.

"So, Tom, is there anything you would like to discuss with me? Your heart appears to be fine, your blood-pressure good, I see that you've managed to keep your weight down too. I'll send off your blood work, but I don't expect to see any surprises there. So how are you feeling in yourself?"

Dr. Carroll was a gentle, old-school type of doctor. He was easy to talk to being a good listener and an overall empathetic person. Unfortunately, he was due to retire soon which made Tom feel agitated. Rose and he had been fortunate to have had Dr. Carroll as their family physician for over fifteen years and he would be sorely missed.

"I generally feel in good physical health, but I am concerned about my memory. I know that as we get older our memories are not as sharp, but my brain often feels sort of jumbled and I forget where I've put things. The term 'losing my mind' is how I would describe I sometimes feel."

Dr. Carroll looked at Tom sympathetically.

"I could send you to the Memory Clinic and get you tested although I personally don't think that is necessary. You sound like ninety percent of my patients over the age of sixty. It's frightening to feel that your brain is not as sharp as it should be but, believe me, it's quite normal. Would you like me to make an appointment for you to be tested for dementia? If you're truly worried about this maybe it would allay your fears."

Tom thought about it and then said that he would like to have the test as one thing that he had learnt in life was that one should face up to one's fears squarely. With that decision made he thanked the doctor and quickly left the clinic. Looking at the time, Tom smiled. He would still manage to get a sail in before supper.

Tranquillity was moored on the north side of the marina just East of The Cottage Colony. Tom parked his car and was about to walk down to the slip to his boat when he noticed a stunningly beautiful woman sitting on the bench overlooking the river. She looked to be in her thirties, although Tom was absolutely hopeless at guessing ages. It was her long, dark hair that hung like two curtains on each side of her face that had drawn his attention to her. She looked like the singer, Crystal Gayle, a blast from the past who had been very popular in the eighties. Tom turned his gaze away from her, but not before she had locked her eyes on him. She called out in a soft, melodious voice, "Do I know you? You look so familiar. By the way, I'm Maddie." She stood up and walked towards Tom and stretched out her slender hand to be shaken.

Tom just stared and then he shook his head and smiled back as he took her hand. "I'm sorry I was a million miles away. I'm Tom, pleased to meet you, Maddie. What brings you to the marina? Do you have a boat here?"

Maddie looked wistfully at the colourful array of boats moored along the quays.

"In my dreams, no, I don't own a boat but I've been sailing all my life, so I know a thing or two about boats. Coming down to the marina connects me to my passion."

Later, Tom would recall this conversation with incredibility. How had he been so gullible and naïve, but he had been so smitten by her stunning looks and romantic manner that all common sense had gone out the window.

"Look," Tom said impulsively, "I'm about to take my boat out for a sail. You can join me if you'd like."

Her smile was enough to warm his heart. She was as eager as a child fairly jumping up and down with unbridled excitement.

"Really, oh Tom, that would be super."

"Come on then, I've got two hours before I need to be home for dinner. How are you off for time?"

"Well, I'm visiting my parents so I suppose that I should be back in time for dinner too. I'm in your hands, Tom."

Tom walked with a spring in his step towards *Tranquillity*, followed very closely by Maddie who couldn't wipe the smile off her face. This was working out exactly as she had planned.

EIGHTEEN

After John's phone call Rose was left feeling decidedly unsettled. When would her foolish heart stop yearning for a man she could never have; it was just ridiculous and adolescent and thoroughly wrong. She decided to bake a cake- it was Rose's go-to whenever she felt stressed. Baking was like a balm to her soul. She would make Tom's favourite chocolate cake.

Opening the fridge to retrieve some eggs, Rose saw that there was a bowl of cooked mince left over from before they went away. She would have to use it that day otherwise Puff and Ben would end up eating if for their dinner. Rose decided to make a meat and potato pie for their dinner. She would make the pastry first and leave it to rest in the fridge while she baked the cake. Pulling out all the ingredients, she assembled them on the work top and proceeded to cream the butter and sugar together and then she beat in the flour, baking powder, cocoa, adding half a cup of their left-over coffee, and lastly, beating in three eggs. When the cake was in the oven, Rose peeled and chopped up the potatoes and put them on to boil. Just then the phone rang.

"Oh, hi Rose, I'm back and I've got tons to tell you. Can I come around now?"

'Of course, if you don't mind the mess, I'm cooking. Yes, come now, I'll make us a pot of tea."

Susan grinned. Her friend loved tea, for herself a glass of wine would go down a treat. Maybe she would bring a bottle around for them to share.

Ten minutes later Rose was just draining off the potatoes when the doorbell rang. Susan had arrived. Rose put the kettle on and went to open the door, Susan stood there with a bottle of wine in her hands, maybe tea would have to wait. Ushering her friend into the kitchen Rose pulled out a stool.

"Just sit here for a minute while I roll out my pastry, Susan. When I've put together the pie and taken out the cake we can go and sit in the sun lounge. Okay?"

Susan liked to watch her friend cook as there was something soothing about the ease in which Rose put things together.

"Now, have I got loads to tell you." Susan said while Rose lined the pie dish with pastry.

"Go on them, don't keep me waiting, I want you to tell me everything. Oh, and I have some news for you as well."

"Okay, so you know that I had dinner with Trevor, well, I asked him about Alex, oh, mean David Grantham and he told me that he had been red flagged on more than one occasion over the years. He's a local Timmins man and has a big house by Hollinger Golf Course and a condo in Florida in Naples Beach. Apparently he got his fingers burnt with some local loan sharks over the proposed new casino. The police have been watching him for years. Now the other interesting piece of information I gleaned from Trevor was that Brian Henderson's wife is actually David Grantham's sister-in-law. She grew up in Timmins, went off to Queens University, met and married Michael Grantham a professor at the university, had a baby girl, and then was widowed after a big scandal involving some of the female students in her husband's faculty. Michael Grantham took his own life. Sylvia and her daughter returned to Timmins where she got a job at Silvercorp as a receptionist. That's where she met Brian Henderson. They married and lived in a house down by the Mattagami River until fifteen years ago when they moved to Bayfield."

Rose had been listening to Susan's story and she hated to burst her friends bubble by telling her that she had already received the same information from John Hargreaves. She decided to play along and pretend that it was all new and exciting news.

"Wow, well I'll be seeing Sylvia at the Croquet Club cocktail party tomorrow. I'll ask her if she went to Queens and see what she answers. So, the daughter, she would have to be in her late forties by now if she was only five when her father died."

Susan looked at Rose quizzically, "Who told you that she was five? I certainly didn't."

Rose laughed, "I can't pull the wool over your eyes, can I? Actually I didn't like to say, but John Hargreaves phoned this morning and gave me all the information that you've just told me yourself, plus some more, like the daughter's name and age, Maddie, and she has to be in her late forties."

Susan looked deep in thought. "So let's get this straight: Sylvia married Michael Grantham, a professor at Queens

University, they had a child together and then he commits suicide leaving Sylvia a widow and a single mother. She returns to her hometown, Timmins, where her brother-in-law gets her a job at the mine as a receptionist. Sylvia meets Brian Henderson, they get married and live in Timmins until Brian retires leaving David to run the mine. Sylvia and Brian move to Bayfield. What happens to the daughter and could she somehow be connected in anyway to the mine? How does Sylvia fit in with all of this? Ah, gee, Rose, there are far more questions than answers here."

The chocolate cake was ready to take out of the oven and the pie all assembled. Rose grabbed a tray, put two wine glasses on it and opened the fridge and pulled out a great slab of cheese. She proceeded to cut some generous wedges, putting these on a plate with crackers and a bunch of grapes.

"Susan, can you bring the wine and I'll carry the tray into our sun-room. Let's sit down and have some wine and continue our conversation in comfort."

NINETEEN

Back in the marina Tom had managed to convince Maddie to put on a lifejacket. He always insisted that anyone, including himself, wore one. He knew that lifejackets saved lives.

Maddie jumped on to the boat and looked around the polished deck and cockpit. She could see that *Tranquillity* had been much loved and cared for by Tom.

"Right, do you want me to take the helm, Tom?"

"Umm... well, first let's get the boat started." Tom put the key into the ignition, leant into the cabin to turn on the batteries, pressed the starter, and after two or three attempts the engine burst into life. After warming it up he set about readying the mooring lines and took the helm to reverse *Tranquillity* out of his slip.

"Could you release those two front mooring lines while I let go of the rear ones?"

Tom put the boat into reverse and carefully manoeuvred it

out of the slip. Once clear of the docks Tom engaged the forward gear and then proceeded to cruise slowly through the narrow entrance into the main river past fishing-trawlers and other working boats.

Tom noticed that Maddie had collected up the ropes and had neatly coiled them at her feet. He watched as she tied her beautiful long hair back into a pony tail. Looking at her again in the bright sunlight, Tom realized that she was indeed older than he had first thought. The fine lines on each side of her eyes and forehead were a give away. She was probably around Jessica's age or older, somewhere in her late forties. Averting his eyes he pointed to the impressive houses on the bluff over looking the lake.

"That's Harbour Lights, lovely homes."

It sounded a bit lame, Tom thought but now that he was on the boat with Maddie he suddenly felt a bit awkward; she was, after all, a complete stranger to him.

They cruised alongside the pier where several men were fishing. It was a perfect afternoon for sailing; he would be able to let the sails perform their magic. They reached the lake and Tom grabbed the jib sail, opening it up to the wind. As the sail took up the wind, *Tranquillity*, gathered speed; soon they were sailing at a rate of knots, a feeling of exhilaration ran through Tom's body. This was what he lived for. He glanced at Maddie who beamed back at him. Tom was about to suggest that she took over when suddenly Maddie grabbed the rudder and pulled violently at the main sail sheet. It all happened so fast, before Tom could shout out a warning the boom hit him hard on his back and the next thing he knew was that his body had become air bound. The splash as he hit the water sounded like glass breaking and fairly sucked the air out of Tom's lungs. The shock of icy water engulfing him made Tom panic. He kicked his legs fiercely and rose to the surface gasping for air. He looked around for the boat. All he could see was *Tranquillity* sailing off into the horizon. Where was Maddie? Surely she would have seen him knocked into the water. Unless, unless....

DCI Hargreaves had spent most of the afternoon on the phone with DI Manning in Timmins. The tailing-pond had been dredged and sure enough, David Grantham's body had been recovered. The pathologist was scheduled to complete the post-mortem that same day, but Trevor could tell John that the man had been shot in the neck and it was not a pretty sight. They would send a copy of the pathologist's report to John, although strictly speaking he should not be sharing the information with the London Serious Crimes Unit as it was out of their jurisdiction.

"I do appreciate what you're doing, Trevor and no, I haven't opened a case file for this, it's your murder. I just have an interest in the consortium angle and the 'accidental deaths' that have occurred here in Huron County. I'll keep you informed of anything that I might uncover. Thanks, mate, great working with you."

After John had put the phone down, he sat there quietly absorbing the information gleaned from Trevor. Shooting someone close up was not for the faint hearted. There would have been an awful lot of blood and in all likelihood the killer would have been quite splattered with blood. Could Brian Henderson have shot the man and then coolly driven back to the mine and then walk into the office as if nothing had occurred? He would surely have to have cleaned up and, likely, changed his clothing. It didn't seem plausible, but if not

Brian, then who else could have murdered David Grantham?"

John grabbed a pen and wrote down all the names of the people associated with Silvercorp. Afterwards he looked at his paltry list and let out a deep sigh. Ruffling his hair with his other hand he drew a big circle around Sylvia and her daughter Maddie. He would look deeper into their pasts and if there was anything at all suspicious, John was confident that he would find it.

Back in Lake Huron, Tom swam and then rested on his back and then repeated the whole process until he was closer to the shore. He knew that he would be able to swim the last 200 metres and that he would come ashore on the north beach just south of Deer Park. He rested a while longer and then with a steady crawl he swam to the shore and flopped on the beach thoroughly exhausted. He lay there for a good five minutes before getting up and trudging over the rise and back down to the north shore marina. Ten minutes later he was back at his slip staring at *Tranquillity* which had been moored up as if she had never left. Sitting on the deck was Maddie checking her phone. Tom, unable to contain his anger shouted at her.

"What did you think that you were doing leaving me in the lake like that? You didn't even attempt to rescue me. What's going on?"

Maddie looked at Tom all wide-eyed and innocent and then spoke softly, "Thank God you're alive. I'll call off the Search and Rescue and tell them you're fine." She proceeded to tap in the number and spoke to the rescue people. "Yes, it's Maddie here. Look, Tom's turned up and he's fine. Thank you for everything."

Tom could feel himself calming down, but he still felt as if something was not right. He was about to tell Maddie to leave when she jumped off the boat and ran over to him throwing her arms around his neck and gave him a big kiss. "Thank you, Tom, that was a fabulous sail. I'll see you around." And with that she walked quickly away and back to the carpark leaving Tom feeling thoroughly gobsmacked.

TWENTY

The next day Rose was in the middle of scrambling some eggs for their breakfast when the phone rang. It was Wendy, the Croquet Club secretary. The cocktail party venue had changed as the Henderson's had unexpectedly had a death in the family and had to go up to Timmins. The Croquet Club cocktail party would now be held at Mary and Jim's house.

Tom ambled into the kitchen still in his pyjamas. He stretched out his arms and yawned loudly.

"Something smells good, love. Is that bacon I can smell cooking?"

"Yes, bacon and scrambled eggs coming up. Oh, by the way, the cocktail party is now being held at Mary and Jim's. Brian and Sylvia have to go back up to Timmins. Someone in their family has died, could that be David Grantham? Wasn't he Sylvia's brother-in-law?"

Tom looked at Rose blankly. "That's the first I've heard of that. Alex, I mean David, is related to Brian and Sylvia, fancy that. You know something, that's probably where he was staying all this time, with the Henderson's."

Rose realized that although John Hargreaves had spoken to her on the phone about Sylvia's first marriage, and she had discussed it with Susan over a glass of wine- she had not told Tom about any of the conversation.

"Oh, I'm sorry darling. I should have told you that John telephoned yesterday and put me in the picture about Sylvia's first marriage to Michael Grantham and how David was her brother-in-law. Susan also gave me the same information as Trevor Manning had filled her in with the news. It appears that your 'Alex' has been on the police radar for years and the proposed Timmins Casino has had him under even more scrutiny. He's been dealing with some scary people, wheeling and dealing with money. Anyway, the man is dead now so you won't have to fear for your life anymore, darling?"

Tom hadn't told Rose about the episode on the boat with Maddie. He was somewhat embarrassed to say the least and didn't want to own up to his stupidity. He had played the whole sailing incident over and over in his mind. Had Maddie deliberately turned the boat causing him to fall into the lake? Tom's gut feelings told him that it had been a planned manoeuvre, but if so, just why?

"Are you alright, Tom? You look miles away? Are you going to play croquet today or not?"

Tom shook his head and told Rose that he had already planned to play golf with Doug. He would go along to the cocktail party later.

"Okay then, I won't make dinner for tonight."

The cocktail parties varied according to the hosts, but generally there was a wonderful buffet provided for the players. It was a great social event and one that Rose looked forward to each week.

It was another beautiful day, perfect for playing golf or croquet. Rose, wearing her white pants and top, soon joined in a game. Jean, Roy's wife and widow, paired up with Janice. She would talk to Jean later at the cocktail party, Rose thought as she prepared to hit her first ball.

A couple of hours later, a glass of wine in her hand and a plate of assorted canapés by her side, Rose managed to corner Jean.

"Jean, how have you been doing?"

Jean looked tired, but she valiantly smiled at Rose.

"Oh, you know, Rose, life goes on. It's already a month since Roy's funeral and I've just about stopped crying every time his name is mentioned. But what about you? I heard that you'd gone up to Timmins to check out the mine?"

That was the problem with living in a small village; everyone knew each others business.

"Yes, Susan and I took a road trip up there and I don't know if we found out anything substantial, but I can tell you that Alex's real name is, or should I say was, David Grantham and he is now dead."

"Good God, much as I despised the man for talking Roy into joining the consortium, I certainly wouldn't wish the man dead. How did he die and why does the name Grantham ring a bell for me?"

"It's an odd story Jean, but the long and the short of it is that David Grantham was Sylvia's brother-in-law."

"You mean our Sylvia, Brian's wife?" Jean said incredulously.

"Yes, I'm afraid so but think back now to our university days. You were at Queen's, weren't you?"

"Yes, yes, you and I were in the same graduating year. What's that got to do with all of this?"

"Can you remember the big scandal with that professor who got caught having relationships with many of his students. His name was Michael Grantham, and he was married to Sylvia. Apparently, when he was fired from the university, he was so humiliated that he took his own life."

"So, when did Sylvia marry Brian then? I thought that they had been married forever."

"Oh, Sylvia had a child from Michael, a little girl who was about five at the time of her father's death. Mother and daughter returned to Timmins where Sylvia had grown up. She got, with a bit of help from her brother-in-law, David, a job working as a receptionist at Silvercorp which is where she met Brian. So, Jean, what do you remember about that scandal? I'm afraid I was so wrapped up in love with Tom that I dropped out of most of my clubs including the drama club that Professor Grantham headed up. Wasn't it the drama club students who blew the whistle on him?"

Jean had gone very still and quiet as she thought back all those years. Yes, she had indeed been one of the drama students and Michael Grantham had tried it on with her. He had been quite persistent and had tried to grope her on more than one occasion. At first she had felt a bit flattered that he had singled her out, but then it felt just plain creepy and she started missing her rehearsals just to avoid seeing him, finally dropping out altogether. Nowadays the me-too movement would have made havoc over the story, the press, even way back then, had been pretty brutal. Jean herself had never officially stepped forward to say that she had been abused, she hadn't thought that it was necessary, the man had not raped her, but she had signed the petition to get him to quit his post. Jean had not heard about his subsequent suicide and now she felt sad that their actions had caused a man to take his own life. She would never have signed the petition all those years ago had she known what the outcome would have been.

"So surely none of what happened at Queens has any bearing on the death of David Grantham, does it?" Jean asked obviously feeling guilty about the part she had played all those years ago.

Rose shook her head, "No, there probably is no connection, but it does seem a coincidence that Sylvia is related to David. The trouble is, Jean, coincidences always set off alarm bells for me. I'm not sure what is going on, but the Timmins police are investigating the murder."

"You didn't tell me that he had been murdered. Gosh, that's terrible. Changing the subject, Rose, but where is Tom? I didn't see him out at the Croquet Courts?"

Rose looked at her watch. It was almost six. Where was Tom? He should have been at the cocktail party by now.

TWENTY-ONE

T om and Doug had enjoyed a brilliant game of golf at The White Squirrel in St. Joseph's. Since the new owners had taken over the facility the greens were immaculate and now, sitting on the beautiful patio looking out over the golf course, Tom felt a great wave of contentment wash over him. The whole business of the Silvercorp mine consortium seemed a million miles away and even the strange boating trip with Maddie had taken on a surreal sense. Doug and he sat down at a table shaded by an umbrella and they ordered a couple of beers.

"Are you going to order a burger, Tom?" Doug asked.

Tom looked at his watch. It was already 3:30, the croquet cocktail party was at 5:00 p.m. and as much as Tom was tempted, he shook his head and declined, "I'll just stick to my beer, but you go ahead and order."

Doug ordered a hamburger and the men sat in amicable silence just taking in the wonderful surroundings. Suddenly, Tom felt someone standing behind him and he noticed Doug's face light up radiantly. He turned around quickly just as he felt a small jab on his shoulder. His quick action of turning rapidly caused the person standing behind him to jump backwards and in doing so she managed to trip on the leg of the chair Tom was sitting on. She had ended up falling to the ground heavily, smashing her head loudly against the concrete paving slab. Tom jumped up and looked at the motionless body just as Doug frantically called for help. The unconscious girl on the ground was none other than Maddie.

"Call the ambulance, Doug," Tom shouted, "I think that she's hit her head rather badly."

The other patrons of the patio had got up and were now peering over to where Maddie lay still on the concrete floor. Tom leant over her and took her wrist to see if he could find a pulse.

"What just happened here?" he asked Doug and then Tom noticed a syringe lying on the ground and he recalled the prick on his shoulder. Was Maddie attempting to inject him with something?

The waiters were huddled around her and the manager too. "We've called for an ambulance," Tom reassured the staff. Turning to Doug, he again asked his friend what had happened?

"Did you see her jab me with a syringe, Doug?"

Doug looked perplexed, "A syringe?"

Tom picked up the syringe off the floor and held it up. "This. I don't think that she succeeded, but did you actually witness her attempt to inject me?"

"Well, all I could see from across the table was a stunningly beautiful woman standing behind you. To be quite honest I was rather mesmerized by her looks; I couldn't see what she was doing. She did look very familiar with you as if she was an acquaintance of yours. Do you know who she is?"

"Yes, her name is Maddie and I swear she tried to drown me yesterday in the lake and today it looks as if she's attempted murder again. As to what she's up to, well, I haven't a clue. I'm sure that the police will have something to say about it."

They could hear the ambulance sirens getting closer and closer and soon they were surrounded by paramedics. Maddie was strapped to a stretcher and carried out to the waiting ambulance. The police arrived just as the paramedics were about to depart. Sergeant Flowers walked over to Doug and Tom.

"So, can you tell us just what happened here?"

Doug went first. "Well, this strange woman came up behind Tom and attempted to inject him with this," he held up the syringe, "and Tom turned around quickly, she stepped backwards and seemed to trip. The next thing we knew she was on the ground lying unconscious."

Sergeant Flowers had been taking notes while Doug had been speaking. He put his pen down and turned to Tom, "Have you anything more to add?"

"Not really. It all happened very fast and really I was unaware that she was even standing behind me until I saw Doug's face light up."

"Do you know her at all?"

"I met her for the first time yesterday at the Bayfield Marina. I was taking my boat out when we struck up a conversation." Tom was reluctant to say anything about the boating incident and so he left it out for the time being.

Another officer had sidled up and proceeded to bag up the

syringe. "Did she have a purse or anything?" he asked Tom and Doug.

"Not that we saw, honestly, it all happened so quickly. You might ask one of the waiters. Maybe she was sitting on the patio enjoying a drink before we came along. Your guess is as good as ours."

Tom looked at his watch and blanched when he saw that it was already past 5:30. Rose would be wondering where the heck he had gone.

"Is that all officer, as I really need to leave. My wife was expecting me at a party half an hour ago."

"Let me just take down your contact information and then you may leave. We'll be in touch the minute that we know anything ourselves."

Tom and Doug gave the police officer their telephone numbers and then left The White Squirrel as quickly as they could. Doug was driving.

"Just drop me off at Mary and Jim Le Croix's house, Doug. I'm awfully late for the cocktail party." Tom said as they reached the outskirts of Bayfield.

TWENTY-TWO

Rose looked at her watch again. It was almost six and the cocktail party was beginning to wind down. There was still no sign of Tom. She wondered if he had just plain and simply forgotten as his memory had truly become quite a concern to her. She was about to leave herself when Jean came up to her again.

"Rose, I've been talking to a few people about the Henderson's. You did know that David Grantham's death was the reason for them cancelling their venue for the cocktail party. Also, did you know that Sylvia's daughter is currently visiting them, and Eileen signed that petition too at Queens all those years ago..."

Rose wasn't interested in gossip and was more focused on going home then chatting any further to Jean. She had pretty well stopped listening to her when suddenly she was bought to attention.

"I beg your pardon Jean, but did you just say that Eileen also signed the petition that led to Michael's resignation?"

"Yes, I thought that you already knew that Eileen and I were at Queens together. You obviously cannot remember us from way back then although I remember you. Didn't you drop out of 'A Midsummers Night's Dream?'"

"Oh yes, you do have a good memory, don't you? Well, if truth be known, I'd fallen in love with Tom and nothing else seemed to matter to me, just Tom. I didn't even know about the petition although I remember how shocked I felt when I heard about Professor Grantham and his relationships with some of his students. I always liked him as he was an excellent lecturer, very passionate about English."

"He was passionate, alright," Jean laughed and then sobered up, "Don't you think that it's rather odd that Eileen, you, and I should all end up being married to three men who all got talked into forming a consortium for Silvercorp? The common denominator is that all of us three women were at Queen's University together and all part of the same drama group. Talk about weird coincidences."

Rose never got to answer Jean as Tom suddenly appeared looking red in the face and flustered.

"Oh, there you are, love. I am so sorry to be late. There was an emergency at the golf course. A young woman fell over and had to be rushed by ambulance to hospital. Doug and I had to wait for the police, and it all took forever."

"Why were the police involved, surely an ambulance would have been enough?"

Tom looked evasive.

"Come on, Tom, spill the beans. What aren't you telling me?"

He looked torn but then Tom decided that Rose deserved to know the truth.

"Well, love, you see the woman tried to kill me and it was a sheer fluke that I turned around just as she was about to inject me with a syringe. She tripped up and ended up hitting her head on the concrete patio."

"Did you know her? Why would she, a stranger, try to kill you, Tom, it doesn't make any sense."

Rose felt her voice rising to the point that people had turned their heads and were looking in their direction.

"Come on, Tom, tell me who she is?"

"Calm down, love. Look, all I know is that she was down at the marina yesterday, and I took her for a sail in *Tranquillity*. She almost capsized the boat leaving me to swim to shore. Then, back in the marina she acted as if it had been one big accident. The next time I saw her was at The White Squirrel where she tried to inject me with something."

"Tom, did she tell you her name?" Rose sounded thoroughly exasperated.

"Yes, she said her name was Maddie."

"Did you say Maddie? Now that's too much of a co-incidence. Jean was just telling me that Sylvia's daughter is called Maddie, actually I think its Madison Grantham and she is staying with them right now."

TWENTY-THREE

John had been working all day searching on the internet. He wanted to know everything there was to know about the Henderson and Grantham families. So far, he had formed a pretty clear picture of Sylvia and Brian. Sylvia was the daughter of Polish immigrants, she married Michael Grantham, moved to Kingston, gave birth to Madison, and was widowed five years later. She returned to her hometown of Timmins where her brother-in-law secured her a job as receptionist for Silvercorp. She met Brian, a mining engineer, they got married, he purchased the mine, and years later they retired to live in Bayfield. On the internet he found a few newspaper articles on the take-over of Silvercorp. Pictures of a handsome man and his pretty wife cutting a ribbon with headlines, *Fresh Blood for Silvercorp*. Over a span of ten years there were the usual headlines mostly charity events that Silvercorp had sponsored with large amounts of money and pictures of Brian Henderson in his capacity of President of the Timmins Rotary Club or on the board of directors of the Timmins hospital. If the newspaper articles were to be believed, the Henderson's were model citizens of the community.

Next, John Googled Madison Grantham and was surprised at what he found. In her profile she was born in Kingston but grew up in Timmins. At the age of eighteen she went off to university where she studied mining engineering. After qualifying, Maddie joined Silvercorp. Five years later, she returned to university and got a law degree. Going back to Silvercorp she worked as their legal advisor. She had likely drawn up the shareholders agreements for the consortiums that Tom and his friends had joined. *Maddie was certainly one smart cookie,* John thought as he turned off his computer ready to leave the office for home. He was about to depart when the phone rang. He looked at the display to see who was calling. It was Clinton OPP officer Sergeant Flowers. John picked up the phone,

"DCI Hargreaves speaking."

"Umm... John, guv, oh what the heck, DCI Hargreaves, it's Sergeant Flowers. I think that we've had an attempted murder here in Huron County. Tom Blair just missed being injected with a lethal solution of potassium chloride."

It had all come out in a rather garbled way and John was finding it difficult to follow, however, at the mention of Tom his ears picked up.

"Slow down, Sergeant. So, where did this incident take place?"

"At The White Squirrel golf clubhouse, on the patio."

"And the perpetrator, have you got him in custody?"

"It's not a 'him' DCI Hargreaves, the perpetrator is a woman, one Madison Grantham."

John almost jumped out of his seat when he heard the name. Hadn't he just been reading all about the smart Madison Grantham? What an uncanny co-incident.

"So, I repeat, is she in custody or not?"

"She's in the intensive care unit at Exeter hospital. When she attempted to inject Tom with the syringe he turned around quickly causing her to trip and fall onto the patio hitting her head badly. She's suffered a massive head trauma and is currently in an induced coma."

"Okay, so she's not going anywhere, but make sure that you have an officer on guard watching her. Have you interviewed Tom Blair? We need to understand the motive for this attempted murder. I tell you what Sergeant, I'll drive over to Bayfield myself tomorrow and talk to the Blairs. I'll copy you into the interview notes, okay?"

John ended the call and stood there deep in thought. Curiouser and curiouser, he thought, the Grantham/Henderson triangle was closing in. He could feel that the case would soon be solved. There were just a few loose ends to tie and he knew that Sergeant Manning in Timmins, would be aptly doing that as he spoke.

TWENTY-FOUR

As soon as Rose found out that Maddie Grantham had twice attempted to take Tom's life, she telephoned her friend Susan Parker.

"I've got loads to tell you, Susan. Can I pop over for a bit, I want to talk without Tom hearing what I have to say, is now okay?"

Susan looked at her watch, it was 7:00 p.m. and Ian Green had said that he might come over later for a drink, not dinner, because he liked to eat dinner with his elderly mother who, at the age of ninety, still cooked a daily meal for them both. Sometimes Susan found it irritating that a grown man should still be living at home with his mother. Other times this aspect of him, she found appealing. It showed that he had a kind and caring heart and as Susan got older that was mostly all that she wished for in a relationship.

"Yes, come now and I'll open a bottle of wine. I've got Ian coming around later but I've got some time before then to catch up with you. I've also got loads to tell you as Trevor

Manning just sent me a detailed report which is very interesting. See you soon."

Rose called out to Tom that she was popping over to Susan's for a short while and he answered that he would take the dogs for a walk and would see her later.

Rose arrived at Susan's condo five minutes later and was greeted effusively by Fluffy the cat. Susan ushered her in to her cosy sitting room where a bottle of chardonnay sat opened next to two wine glasses.

"Right, you go first, Rose. What have you got to tell me?"

"Well, Sylvia Henderson's daughter has twice tried to kill Tom, first when he took her out for a sail on *Tranquillity*, and then again today at The White Squirrel Clubhouse. She has to be involved in all of this, but I'm not sure exactly why."

Susan had been listening to her friend incredulously. She, herself had just received a long and detailed report from Trevor Manning about the Henderson family and a large part of the report dealt with the daughter, Madison Grantham. She did not, however, have her pegged for a murderer.

"Okay, Rose, let's try and look at all the facts and see if we can make sense of what we now know. So, number one, it seems to all start in Kingston with Dr. Michael Grantham misbehaving himself with some students and then getting himself fired. That is a fact on record."

Rose interrupted Susan, "Yes, and also on record is the petition signed by the students who he had abused including Eileen, Jean, and myself although I was never actually taken advantage of so technically I shouldn't have signed the petition, but don't you think that it's just too much of a coincidence that the name's on the petition have been maligned..."

Susan stopped Rose mid-sentence. "You're getting ahead

of yourself Rose, let's just stick to the facts. So, we have the professor fired from Queens and then he takes his own life. Sylvia and Maddie, age five, move back to Timmins. Now this is what was in the long report Trevor sent me. Maddie and her mother fell on hard times. The little girl displayed psychotic behaviour and was in and out of Children's Aid and at one stage she was in foster care for a whole year. The only good thing was that Maddie appeared very smart and she always attended school. The same year that Sylvia met Brian in 1990, Maddie had turned the corner and was winning scholarships left, right, and centre. Two years later she went off to university to study mining engineering. Sylvia married Brian and they all seemed to live happily ever after, ha, ha, but we're dealing in facts so let's move on to the brother-in-law, David Grantham and see where he fits in with all of this.

"According to Trevor, David and Michael as brothers were like polar opposites. Born to British immigrants the two attended the local high school, but whereas Michael knuckled down and worked studiously, David played around and left school at sixteen to work in the mine. When the mine closed in the 1980s, he went out west to Saskatchewan where he fell on hard times. We don't know much about this period of his life other than the fact that there is no record of employment. David did however return to Timmins seemingly a wealthy man and was back in time for the opening of the mine under new ownership. Brian Henderson now owned Silvercorp, Sylvia worked as the receptionist, David as his right- hand man, and Maddie, on graduation, also worked for Silvercorp. It was beginning to look like a real family affair."

Rose interrupted Susan again, "Right, let's return to the facts as we know them. I gather Maddie went back to university to study law. When did David Grantham start up the Silvercorp consortiums and how many of them were formed?"

"Good questions, Rose," Susan said as she read the detailed report from Trevor looking for the answers. "Right, here we are, Madison Grantham rejoined Silvercorp as their mining lawyer and legal advisor in 2012. It appears the first consortium was formed a couple of years later in 2014, the second in 2016 and the third in 2018, pretty well every two years one was formed. Trevor has a list of names of all the shareholders if we want to see if we can recognize anyone."

Susan handed Rose a list of names; there were twelve in total and she immediately recognized George, Roy, Tom, and Alex's names. The other names didn't ring any bells although one, a Tony Mellor, sounded vaguely familiar to Rose.

"The trouble is Susan, if our theory is right the girls that signed the petition all those years ago have long since been married to men we've never heard of. It would be so much easier if we had the wives' names as well."

"I'm sure that would be easy enough to search," Susan said, "So you're still going down the route of some sort of vengeance theory, but why after all these years? What we need to check out though is how many of the men in the consortiums died and how they died. There again, with a little research I'm sure we will be able to get answers to these questions and quite quickly too. It does seem pretty coincidental that the consortiums were all formed after Maddie became Silvercorp's lawyer and you know how I hate coincidences."

Rose was very quiet. She had found it hard to believe that Maddie would set out to destroy the lives of so many families just to seek retribution for her mother. But she also knew how one couldn't always rationalize the motives of someone with mental health issues and it truly sounded as if Maddie was verging on psychopathic. If it wasn't for the attempts on Tom's life she might have dismissed their hypothesis as unrealistic and too far-fetched, but the woman obviously had been hell bent on murdering Tom. The awful truth was how close she had come to succeeding in her mission. *I could have been widowed like Jean and Eileen,* Rose thought and let out a soft moan.

"Are you alright, Rose?" Susan asked looking at her friend anxiously.

"Sorry, I was just realizing what a close call it was with Tom. That Maddie must be crazy or possessed, probably both. One thing for certain though is she is one determined lady. Do you know if she's come out of her coma yet?"

"No, but a call to Sergeant Flowers might answer that question. I would also like to find out if the toxicology report has come through yet. Okay, Ian will be here any minute now so I'm going to have to say goodbye to you Rose. I'll make that phone call to Sergeant Flowers tomorrow and see if Trevor can chase down the names of the spouses on that list of consortium shareholders. I'll call you tomorrow, okay?"

Rose got up and smiled. She had been dying to hear about Susan's evening spent with Trevor Manning in Timmins, but it didn't seem quite appropriate to be discussing that when Ian Green was about to arrive. She did, however, just love the way Susan took charge of the situation as if she was still working for the Serious Crimes Unit in London. Rose knew that they would have the answers to their questions within twenty-four hours.

Just as Rose was driving away a black Ford pick-up truck pulled into the guest parking space outside Susan's condo just vacated by Rose. Dr. Ian Green jumped down from his truck, grabbed a bunch of flowers and a tray of eggs from the back seat and walked to Susan's front door with a smile on his face and a bounce in his step. Ian still couldn't believe his good fortune, to be dating the legendary Susan Parker was something he had dreamt about but never for a single minute thought would come true. She was his theme for a dream in every way possible, he just had to pinch himself every now and then to make sure it was all real. The only trouble was they had not progressed beyond first base and Ian wasn't quite sure how to proceed without appearing too pushy. His mother had always driven home the fact that 'manners maketh a man' and he had always tried to practise that creed and as a consequence was super polite and caring towards Susan. Every now and then he had the urge to sweep her up in his arms and ravage her passionately. The trouble was that he wasn't even sure if she even fancied him sexually although when they kissed, he could definitely feel the chemistry between them. Ian also knew that he tended to overthink everything, so he shook his head and knocked on Susan's door. He would let Susan take the lead on their relationship and he would follow.

Susan opened the door and welcomed Ian into her condo. He handed her some beautiful flowers and a large tray of eggs which made her laugh. How many guys had she known who would present eggs as a gift to her? She thanked Ian and led him through into the sitting room.

"Would you like a glass of wine Ian or maybe a beer?"

Ian had immediately noticed the opened bottle of chardonnay and two wine glasses sitting on the coffee table.

"Have you had visitors?" he asked holding up the two wine glasses.

"Oh, my friend Rose just popped in for a chat and I opened a bottle of wine. You probably passed her in the car-park, she literally left two minutes ago."

Susan poured out some wine for Ian and emptied some chips into a bowl. She sat down on the sofa next to him curling up her legs like a cat which was when Fluffy, her kitten, appeared and without warning, jumped up onto Ian's lap so suddenly that he spilt his wine all over himself.

"Oh Ian, I'm so sorry." Susan grabbed Fluffy and shut her in the study, she then went into the kitchen to fetch a cloth to wipe up the spilt wine.

"Here we are, let me try to mop this wine off you before it stains. Thank goodness it's white, not red wine."

Susan began patting Ian's shirt with the cloth and then moved down to his trouser legs. She could hear his breathing alter and then she felt his hands pulling her into his chest. The next thing she knew they were kissing each other so passionately Susan could hardly breath. Ian started to kiss her neck and then he slowly moved down her body. Susan pulled her t-shirt off and grabbed Ian's shirt buttons feverishly trying to undo them. Soon they were lying semi naked on the floor, neither of them had said a single word. Ian methodically continued kissing every inch of Susan's body until she began to shiver and let out a deep and hungry groan.

"Enough, Ian, take me now," and with that Susan grabbed at his pants and pulled so hard that the button burst off. Ian helped her by wriggling his pants down. He lifted Susan up and laid her gently down on the sofa and then he rode her like a stallion and they made deep, passionate, and fulfilling love. Ian's dreams had finally come true.

TWENTY-FIVE

It was a dazzlingly beautiful summer's morning when DCI John Hargreaves drove to Bayfield to interview Tom and Rose Blair. As he drove through Lucan and then Exeter he was reminded of the previous year when he had spent several weeks pursuing the murderer of the hermit scientist who lived by the Bayfield River. Then he had checked into The Little Inn and, after being firmly rejected by Rose, had begun to date her sister, Kate. Their relationship had blossomed and now he was considering proposing to her. He never, however, would forget his first wife, mother of their daughter Rachel, the reason for him moving from England to Canada. These past six years had seen him widowed, become a grandfather, retired from the Metropolitan Police in London, emigrated, and then employed as DCI of the Serious Crimes Unit in London, Ontario. He certainly had had no time to let the grass grow beneath his feet, but he had no regrets. Moving to Canada with its wonderful lifestyle and warm, loving people, had been the best thing John could have done. Compared to the Met, working for Serious Crimes in London was a breeze and he had the added bonus of precious time to visit his daughter and grandson and to generally enjoy life, something that he was surely deprived of before coming to Canada.

John turned left when he reached Brucefield and began the last leg of his journey driving through Varna and then he could see Lake Huron and his heart gave a little lurch. This was where he wanted to be, on the lake in the sleepy village of Bayfield.

He had phoned Tom before setting off so he knew that his visit would not come as a surprise, he also knew that Rose would feel uncomfortable and maybe he could excuse her and just talk to Tom. Pulling into their driveway, John immediately heard Puff and Ben bark; *they were good guard dogs*, he thought as the front door was opened by Rose. She stood there looking like a startled deer.

"Oh, John, you're early. Tom's still getting up. I'll tell him you're here. Come in, I'll put the kettle on for coffee or would you prefer tea?"

John entered and said that coffee would be fine. He looked around their cosy kitchen and then surreptitiously glanced at Rose. She seemed to have aged noticeably over the past year. Fine lines appeared etched on her forehead and her blonde hair now was peppered with grey. It made John feel sad thinking about getting older, after all Rose couldn't be much older than he as she was two years older than her sister who was in turn two years older than John. *If I returned to England would people think that I'd aged*, John thought to himself.

Rose made up a tray with three mugs, a coffee bodum, and a plate of orange and cranberry scones. She carried this through to the sunroom.

"Just sit here while I chivvy Tom along. He won't be long, I promise."

"There's no rush Rose, just sit down yourself and we can talk while Tom gets himself ready."

Rose took a seat opposite John and leant forward to pour out the coffee, handing the mug over to John she said, "I am finding this all very stressful, John. Driving up to Timmins and then coming back to find Tom's life so precariously in the balance. I don't feel very safe anymore."

Tears had started to well up in her eyes and John was a huge sucker for tears. He stood up and walked over to Rose. He wanted to take her in his arms and kiss away her tears, she looked so sad and vulnerable. Just then Tom appeared in the doorway looking somewhat dishevelled and sleepy.

"Sorry John, I overslept this morning, didn't think that you would be here so early. Oh, I see Rose has made some coffee, great, so, let's get started, I've got a game of golf in an hour."

"That's fine, Tom," John said, "I'm meeting Sergeant Flowers later this morning in Clinton, but I do have some questions for you. Now, you told the Sergeant that the accused had made a prior attempt on your life before the incident at The White Squirrel?"

"Yes, I met her at the marina." Tom said quietly, "and I took her for a quick sail in my boat. She was so friendly and desperate to go sailing," *and beautiful too*, Tom thought, but didn't say. "Anyway, she obviously knew how to sail and when we were out into the lake, she just grabbed the jib sail suddenly causing the boat to turn rapidly and almost capsize. I was hit in the back by the boom and knocked into the water. Fortunately, I was able to swim to the shore, but she didn't try to rescue me and I'm convinced it was a deliberate act. She was trying to kill me. Then, the next day she tried again this time with a syringe. Have you had the results of the toxicology back yet?"

John nodded, "Yes, Sergeant Flowers sent me the report yesterday. It appears that the syringe was full of potassium chloride. Had she succeeded you would have had what would appear to have been a heart attack. It would probably have even escaped detection and she would have gotten away with murder. What I don't understand though, is her motive for murder? To attempt to kill you twice shows one determined woman."

"Well actually, I have had several attempts made at my life over the past couple of weeks. I know that it was probably Alex, umm... I mean David Grantham, in his Lincoln Navigator who tried to run me over. It does beg the question, were uncle and niece in collusion together and then where does that leave the mother, Sylvia? Where does she fit in?"

"Those are all good points, Tom. Right now we're treating this as an attempted murder. Ms. Grantham will be charged accordingly when she comes out of her coma. As to David Grantham, well his body has been formerly identified. As far as the perpetrator of his murder, it appears DI Manning has some leads which he is following up. I don't think that his death has any bearing on this case."

Tom looked flabbergasted, "What about Brian Henderson? I thought that he was your prime suspect?"

"Yes, we did have him pegged as highly suspect, but no, I can't tell you for certain, but we have ruled him out."

"Well, was he involved in the consortiums?" Rose asked.

"He says that David and Maddie headed up the consortiums and that he left them to it. We contacted the Henderson's to let them know that their daughter was in critical care. They're flying back from Timmins today and so I'll be interviewing them both tomorrow."

"Well, I can't believe that he's innocent. Why did he lock Susan and I in the storeroom? No, he's not telling you the truth, I just know it."

"You're probably right, Rose, but for now I can only deal with the facts. Tom, can you go through the whole incident at The White Squirrel as I need to officially record this interview. I'm putting my phone on the coffee table."

Tom looked a bit taken aback. "I feel like a criminal, John. Why do you have to record this interview? I'm the victim here not the perpetrator."

John patted Tom on his shoulder, "Look, I don't have to record this but it just makes it easier to transcribe later when the case goes to court."

"Court, why would this go to court?" Tom said indignantly. "That blasted woman tried to kill me and there's no way she could get off the hook for that. Good God, you've got proof in the contents of that syringe, what more could you ask for?"

"Yes, and I totally agree with you, but mark my words we're dealing with a lawyer here and when she recovers from her head trauma she will come at us with everything she can muster. We have to make a solid case of attempted murder with absolutely no loopholes. You must be able to see that? Now, the other incident on your boat we will find very hard to prove that it was anything other than an accident. At least with the botched syringe there were several witnesses and of course, the syringe itself."

Tom understood the reasoning, but he still bristled at being interviewed and recorded like a criminal.

"Okay, John said, "Let's start at the beginning with your game of golf...."

TWENTY-SIX

Maddie Grantham was in a deep coma, her head held in a vice-like contraption, her jet-black hair swept in two curtains on each side of her face. She looked peaceful and at rest, her skin as pale as alabaster and her lips rosy, red like cherries. Snow White came to mind when John looked down upon her still form. *How could someone so beautiful, potentially be so evil,* he thought and then laughed at the absurdity of his own question. History had shown how many evil people had been wolves in sheep's clothing. Could it be that Maddie, smart as she was, suffered from extreme mental health problems? The report from DCI Manning had said that as a child she had suffered from multiple psychotic episodes. Could these episodes have developed into adulthood? John sighed and left the hospital room feeling once again that he had more questions than answers. Maybe the search of Maddie's condo in Timmins might reveal a possible motive for her bizarre actions. He would have to wait to hear from Trevor and his team, but in the meantime he had a meeting set with Sergeant Flowers in Clinton.

Driving from Bayfield to Clinton once again sparked off memories from the previous year's case when John and his team had spent two weeks chasing down the murderer of the eccentric scientist. As he drove down Bayfield Road he could see the Windmill from the eco-park, and he wondered how the owner was doing. He had been so impressed with the Windmill Lake Eco-Park and had told everyone about it and had even promised to take his daughter Rachel wakeboarding one day that summer.

Reaching the small town of Clinton, John was pleasantly surprised to see the town thriving. They had built a new fire hall as well as an amazing new OPP station which now replaced the old one on Highway 21 close to Goderich. The town had also a wonderful community YMCA centre and arena, a college campus which offered satellite programs from Fanshawe College and offered one of the few equine-management courses in the whole of Ontario. If that wasn't enough, the town sported a hospital, several high schools and elementary schools, there was the casino, and the racetrack. It never ceased to amaze John why a town so well endowed with excellent facilities should still struggle to grow. The problem was the main street offered little in terms of good shops and restaurants so there was nothing to draw people in to visit the town other than to go to the casino or racetrack, neither of which necessarily attracted the right kind of people.

John pulled into the OPP car park and got out of his car. The glazed atrium entry was ultra modern. He was greeted by a friendly receptionist.

"Can I help you?"

"Yes, I am DCI Hargreaves and I have a meeting with Sergeant Flowers." John said looking around the shiny entrance way.

"His office is just down the corridor, two doors down. His name is on the door."

John followed her instructions and was soon sitting in a comfortable office furnished with modern IKEA like furniture. Sergeant Flowers sat behind his desk with a wad of paper in front of him.

"I printed this off for you. It's the toxicology report and a copy of the interviews conducted at the scene of the crime. Not an awful lot there but at least we have a few witnesses which is good. The toxicology report shows beyond doubt that the syringe was full of a lethal dosage of potassium chloride which, had it been injected, would have killed Tom Blair instantly. We cannot interview the perpetrator as she is still in a coma. Did you get to interview Tom Blair?"

John went through the interview by playing the recorded version so that Sergeant Flowers could hear it first-hand.

"I'll get this transcribed and written up today and back to you for your records. I'm still not sure of the motive for murder in this case. DCI Trevor Manning up in Timmins is conducting a search of Ms. Grantham's apartment to see if he can find some incriminating evidence which might shed some light on the motive. I'll let you know if they find anything."

"It's a strange case," Sergeant Flowers mused. "We have so few murders in Huron County that it is something of an anomaly. Thank God she didn't succeed in her quest to kill Tom Blair."

"Too right," John said. "Right, well I'll be getting along now back to London although I will be back again tomorrow to interview the Henderson's. They might be able to shed some light on their daughter's strange behaviour."

John drove back to London deep in thought. He hoped to have some answers from DCI Manning before he interviewed the Henderson's.

TWENTY-SEVEN

Ian Green woke with a start. He was in Susan's bed and tangled up in her sheets. Susan herself lay asleep beside him, her hair tousled, and her face still flushed from their love making. After the first burst of passion they had crept upstairs, and this time had made slower love exploring each others bodies in a gentle, less frenzied manner. Then they had both fallen asleep and now Ian looked at his watch and jolted upright. It was almost 7:00. His mother would be frantic, not to mention the chickens who were always fed at 6:30 each morning. He looked down again at Susan and was so tempted to make sweet, sweet love again, but he resisted the urge and instead got up out of bed. Finding his clothes in a jumbled mess on the living room floor he quickly dressed himself and left Susan's condo as quietly as he could. He would phone her later and explain why he had to leave in such a rush. It did feel wrong though and Ian was really torn, but his responsibilities on the egg farm won and so he drove off in the direction of Porters Line as fast as he could.

Susan woke up a while later and looked at the messed-up bed and then remembered Ian and her making sweet love on and off throughout the night. She couldn't stop smiling as she recalled Ian's surge of passion. Still waters truly ran deep she thought as she sat up and looked around for Ian. *He was probably in the bathroom*, she thought as she reached for her robe. Maybe the two of them could go and have a soak in the hot-tub, Susan thought as she went through to the bathroom and found no evidence of the man she had just spent the night making sweet love to. Padding downstairs she quite expected to be greeted by Ian making them both coffee, but no, there was no sign of him anywhere. Susan began to feel angry. It felt so wrong that he should disappear without even saying goodbye particularly after feeling so close to him. Susan sighed. She had been let down before by insensitive men, but she had never dreamt that Ian Green would be one of them.

Hundreds of miles north of Bayfield, Trevor Manning got up and made himself a cup of coffee. He put two pieces of bread in the toaster and poured out some cornflakes into a bowl. He was deep in thought and still feeling overwhelmed by the previous day's discovery. Yesterday he had taken two of his officers with him to search Ms. Grantham's apartment which was located in one of the best parts of the town and was obviously quite an expensive unit of accommodation. The caretaker had let them in so they hadn't had to break the lock which was always better in terms of damage control. The minute they entered Trevor just knew that they had hit a jack-pot. All along the living room were pictures and maps with arrows connecting in different directions. The photographs were of men, mostly men that looked to be in their sixties or seventies. Eight of the pictures had big crosses marked across them. There were two pictures unscathed, one of them Trevor recognized as Tom Blair. There was also a list of women's names pinned next to the photographs of the men. Trevor took out his phone and proceeded to take pictures of the whole wall. Leaving the living room, the team moved into the kitchen. There on the counter was a glass jar labelled potassium chloride. Trevor took a picture of that and then went back to the living room to study the wall again. The whole thing was like a plan of action or like an investigation chart with its flow arrows. One of the pieces of paper pinned to the wall was a petition. It was written out by hand on Queen's University headed paper. There were twelve names, all women, petitioning for the removal of Professor Grantham from the faculty. Trevor read through the list of names and saw Rose's name halfway down. *So, Tom and Rose Blair were on Ms. Grantham's hit list,* Trevor thought.

"Boss, come and look in here." Constable Miller called out. He was in the bedroom.

Trevor walked over towards the open plan kitchen to the master bedroom which was located to the left of the living room. Constable Miller was standing by the side of a king-sized bed looking down at a ten by eight photo of David Grantham framed in an ornamental gilded picture frame. On the wall opposite the bed was a large, framed photograph of Sylvia, Maddie, and presumably her father, Michael Grantham. The little girl in the picture could only have been about four years old. The picture had been taken not long before Michael had taken his own life. There were other pictures of David Grantham and Maddie together and, even though he had to be almost twenty years her senior, they made a handsome couple. He was her uncle and so maybe their relationship was just that, uncle, and doting niece, but looking at the photographs one would have to have been a fool not to think that the two people posing together were not romantically involved. It was of course, verging on incest, Trevor thought, but then throughout history there was nothing about family members marrying, certainly the Royal family lay testament to that.

"Boss, come and look in here." Once again Constable Miller called Trevor over to look inside Maddie's wardrobe. On a shelf stacked with folded sweaters lay a hand-held pistol, a small compact Beretta.

"Could this be the gun used to kill David Grantham, boss?" Constable Miller asked.

Trevor shook his head. No, according to ballistics the gun used to shoot David Grantham in the neck was an Eastern European Luger 27. The bullet extracted from David's neck was a Ukrainian brand very different from the ammunition used in the small Beretta found in Maddie Grantham's wardrobe. It was interesting though, that she should own a firearm. Did she feel unsafe and if so, why?

"Take photographs of everything, Constable and I'll see you back at the station." Trevor said as he took one last look around the room and then departed. He had never for once thought that Maddie Grantham had murdered David Grantham. Trevor was almost sure that he knew who the murderer was and he would hopefully have confirmation of this by the end of the day if all went to plan.

"Tom, have you booked anything for our stay in Kingston?"

It was only two days away and Rose was beginning to feel anxious again about Tom. He should have been acting more relaxed now that both David and Maddie Grantham were out of action, one permanently and the other indefinitely. The threat to his life from so called accidents had been eliminated and he should have been celebrating not going around with such a hang-dog expression. She worried about him and would be pleased when his memory test was over and done with. It had been booked for that afternoon. She repeated her question to Tom who had appeared from his study.

"What did you say, love?"

Rose snorted and repeated herself for the third time.

"Oh yes, well I thought that we would just check into a Holiday Inn. It's pretty central and we can get free parking. I don't think that we need book it in advance."

"I would rather that we did book it, Tom. You know how busy Kingston gets in the summer."

"Alright, I'll book just one room with two doubles if it makes you happy."

"What time is your appointment at The Memory Clinic today, Tom?"

"Good, God, I forgot all about that." Tom said with a twinkle in his eye, "Only joking, love, my appointment is at 2:00 p.m. Are you going to come with me?"

"Yes, I thought I'd come and sit in on it with you. You'll be fine, Tom. I think that you're just stressed out, that's all."

Tom smiled. He wished that he felt as confident as Rose, but still, it would be good to get the test over and done with as there was nothing worse than waiting.

"Right, I'll leave you to book The Holiday Inn while I go and take the dogs for a walk. Maybe we could have lunch in Goderich before your appointment? What do you think, Tom?"

"That would be great love. Okay, I'll go and book the room and then we should leave before noon."

Rose nodded as she called the dogs and grabbed their leashes off the hall table.

"See you later, darling."

TWENTY-NINE

DCI Hargreaves drove back to Bayfield that morning and whereas the previous day the sun had shone and the sky was an azure blue, today the weather had turned and although it was still warm, the sky was grey, and it felt like it might rain. *What a difference a day makes,* John thought as he reached the village and proceeded to drive to Brian and Sylvia Henderson's house on Christy Street. He would have to go lightly with the two of them as losing a brother-in-law and business partner was one thing but coming home to their daughter in a coma having been charged with attempted murder, was altogether quite another matter. John pulled into their driveway and looked at the impressive house before him. It actually looked like two separate houses, maybe one was Maddie's, who knew, but he would soon find out.

Brian Henderson opened the door to John. Although they had met at Silvercorp it was only briefly and John could see that the man was trying to remember his name.

"DCI Hargreaves, sir, I hope that I'm not too early for your interview?"

It was only 9:00 a.m. and after yesterday's interview at the Blair's house he realized that many people in Bayfield were not early risers like himself. Just because he always got up at 6:30 a.m. each day didn't mean other people embraced his early morning regime.

"Come into the kitchen, Sylvia has just made some coffee and there are fresh croissants if you would like one."

Sylvia was an attractive woman probably in her late sixties although she looked at least ten years younger. Maybe it was her hair which she wore to her shoulders, but there was definitely a strong resemblance to her daughter, Maddie whom he had just seen the day before in the hospital. Sylvia stood up when John entered the kitchen and stretched out her hand to him to be shaken.

"Nice to meet you, DCI Hargreaves, please join us for breakfast."

John pulled up a chair and sat down. The kitchen was vast, all marble and granite with a huge island in the middle.

"I won't keep you both too long, but I do have to ask you a few questions about your daughter."

Brian and Sylvia nodded, and John continued.

"I will be recording our interview," here John laid down his phone on the kitchen table next to the plate of croissants, "Okay, let's get going. Sylvia, I believe that Madison was born in Kingston. Can you tell me about her childhood?"

Sylvia looked at Brian and then fidgeted with the pearl necklace that she was wearing.

"Umm... Detective Hargreaves, you probably know about her father's death. Maddie was only five at the time. We moved back to Timmins shortly after Michael's death. If it hadn't had been for David, Michael's brother, I don't know quite what I would have done. He got me a job at the mine where he was working, and Maddie started school and then our troubles began." Sylvia paused and once again looked at Brian.

"This was long before I had met Brian. David became a father figure to Maddie, and everything would have been just fine had the mine not closed down. Silvercorp went into liquidation and David, now unemployed, moved out west to Saskatchewan leaving Maddie and me behind in Timmins. I'm afraid that losing not one, but in effect, two fathers sent Maddie over the edge. She started having psychotic episodes, shouting, screaming, and throwing things around. It got so bad that Children's Aid got called in and I had to admit that I couldn't cope. There followed a period of five years of hell and then, when Maddie was thirteen she began to love school. She became obsessed with her studies and her psychosis seemed to disappear. She academically out shone all her fellow classmates. At the age of seventeen she was awarded a scholarship to Calgary University, all expenses paid. She studied mining engineering. By the time that I met Brian and Silvercorp had been re-opened, Maddie was in her final year at university. David had returned from out west to work for Brian and everything seemed great. Brian and I got married just after Maddie's graduation and she joined the mine that same year."

John interrupted her, "What about her relationship with her uncle after he returned?"

"David and Maddie became very close. There was sixteen years difference in their ages, but that didn't seem to matter. Brian and I tried to talk some sense into the girl, but she wouldn't listen. She went from David being a father substitute to him being her lover. The trouble with Maddie is she is very headstrong and when she gets it into her head that she wants something nothing in the world can change her mind. That was partly why Brian and I decided to move away. David and Maddie seemed to want to run the mine and their lives the way that they wanted, regardless of anyone else. Don't get me wrong, I love my daughter very much, but her obsessive personality is hard to live with. She has mental health issues and, although she is brilliant, she could be a danger to herself and to other people too."

Sylvia's eyes had started to well up. Brian put his arm around her shoulders and squeezed her gently. John looked uncomfortable as he forged on with his questioning.

"The Silvercorp consortiums, were they your daughter's idea or David's?"

Sylvia looked blank, "I know nothing about the business side of Silvercorp. Maybe Brian could answer that question for you?"

Brian sat up straight and looked John in the eyes.

"You have already asked me about those confounded consortiums, and I answered then as I will answer now that David and Maddie were in charge of setting them up. Don't forget that I've been retired from the business for fourteen years now, I just go up once or twice a month to attend the odd meeting or two, but I am still the major shareholder in the corporation. What I can tell you is that Madison had everything sewn up tight on the legal front, everything to do with Silvercorp was above board and legal, I made sure of that."

John paused before asking his next question. "In the event of the shareholders demise I believe the agreement states that the shares are inherited by the remaining share holders in the consortium. What happens when all the consortium members die? Who gets the shares then?"

"Well, that's an easy one to answer; in the event of all four members of the consortium dying, then all the capital shares go back into the company, in this case, Silvercorp. It was all written up in the shareholder's agreement."

"So, none of the relatives would benefit at all?" John said incredulously.

Brian looked ruffled. "Look, detective, how many times do I have to say that it was all legal. If the consortium share-holders had read the whole contract they would have seen with their own eyes the terms and agreements. Believe me, it's all standard procedure."

John didn't know enough about corporate law to dispute it but somehow none of it sounded fair to the family of the deceased particularly after a hefty investment of $200,000.

"So, just as an example, Tom Blair is the only remaining surviving member of the consortium. Does that mean that he inherits all $800,000 of shares?"

Brian smiled and clapped his hands together. "You're catching on now, but in fact Tom's investment and that of his fellow consortium members has actually increased three times in value. The $800,000 is now worth $2.4 million. Tom Blair is one hell of a rich man and he doesn't even know it yet."

John whistled softly through his teeth. It didn't put Tom in a good light, if he hadn't had known the man he would now possibly be the prime suspect for all the murders. No, he was fairly convinced that David Grantham and Maddie were responsible for all the 'accidental deaths' and John also felt pretty sure that he knew who had killed David, he was just waiting on the Timmins police to provide him with the evidence.

There seemed little point in asking any more questions as it was clear that Sylvia knew nothing about the business side of things and Brian, well, he was acting innocent of all knowledge of the consortiums, but John felt that it was just a front. He knew far more than he was letting on. John would just have to wait now to hear back from DC Manning before questioning Brian Henderson again.

THIRTY

Rose and Tom had a relaxing lunch down by the lake at The Station Restaurant in Goderich. Although it was a dull day, it was still warm and they were able to get an outside table on the patio. Looking out over the lake and over towards the salt mine, Rose knew a little about the history of the mine as some years ago Tom and she had gone on a tour. They had stopped the public tours now but then it had been a huge adventure. The present mine, Sifto, was formed in 1950 but Compass Minerals, an American company, had acquired it in the 1990's. It was known to be the largest underground salt mine in the whole of Canada. The original owners were Samuel Platt and Peter McEwen who had been drilling for oil in Goderich in 1866. At 944 feet they had tapped into the Great Michigan Salt Bed, one of the largest and purest salt deposits in the world. The salt boom had an immediate impact on the town of Goderich which, by 1871 was producing thousands of barrels of salt a day. The town became a prosperous centre of commerce very largely due to the salt. There had been other salt mines in and throughout Huron County particularly around Clinton but none of the other salt mines compared in quality to the pure white crystal quality of the Sifto salt. Thinking about the mine made Rose realize just how much the town of Timmins must have relied on the silver mines found in that area. Just like Sifto, Silvercorp employed hundreds of workers and those same employees needed houses, shops, and a decent quality of life. Take the mine away and the livelihood of all those people would be greatly at stake.

"You seem deep in thought, love?" Tom said.

"Oh, I was just thinking about the salt mine and then I started to think about Silvercorp and the town of Timmins. Remember when Volvo pulled out of Goderich and how that impacted the town and the economy. The same would be true if the salt mine should close. Didn't Silvercorp get closed down in the early 1970s? Sylvia would have been living back there then and it must have been a pretty depressing time for everyone in the town."

Their lunch was served and they both ate their meal in companionable silence. Tom looked at his watch. They would have to leave soon to get to his appointment at The Memory Clinic on time.

Twenty minutes later Tom and Rose were ushered into the doctor's surgery. Dr Walsh, according to her name tag, appeared to be a cheery woman probably in her late fifties. She had a no-nonsense way about her, yet her smiley face belied her officious manner. She stood up when the Blair's entered and pointed brusquely to two chairs the other side of her cluttered desk.

"I see that you've come along presumably for moral support, Mrs. Blair. I would appreciate it if you would remain completely silent throughout the procedure, if you don't mind."

Rose nodded and waited for the doctor to continue.

"Some of the questions that I will be asking you Tom, might seem ridiculously easy, but believe me there is a rationale for all of them. So, let's get started. First, I'm going to give you a small written test, mostly clock-faces and filling in the big and little hands to tell the correct time. So here you are." She handed Tom a piece of paper and a pencil. "Take your time and don't rush it."

Tom placed the paper on the edge of the doctor's desk as he couldn't find another hard surface to rest on. He should have been given a clipboard or something like that to write on. *Oh well,* he thought, *this will have to do,* but he didn't like the fact that Dr Walsh could watch him as he answered the questions.

Most of the diagrams on the sheet of paper were, as the good doctor had predicted, of clock faces. He had to draw in the hands for 3:40, 5:30, and 9:45. That was easy enough. The next question Tom had to think a minute before answering, name the colour sequence of traffic lights: red, green, orange, and red. Next, he had to write down the numbers from one to twenty but backwards starting with twenty. Then the dates, what date was it yesterday, what will it be tomorrow, in four days time? By the end of the test Tom was convinced that he had answered everything right. He handed the test paper over to Dr. Walsh.

She glanced through it and then started to fire questions at him.

"What year is it, Tom?"

"What year was it last year?"

"Count backwards from 30 to 1."

All the questions seemed simple to Tom and he felt that there had to be a trick question lurking waiting to trip him up. But no, after twenty-five minutes of testing, Dr. Walsh smiled at Tom and Rose and declared that Tom was one hundred percent okay.

"But what about my forgetfulness?" Tom asked.

"Most of that is just part of getting old. However, stress can play a major part in this so I suggest that you try to destress your life if at all possible. What about exercise? Do you exercise regularly, Tom?"

"Well, I play golf at least four times a week and I take the dogs for a walk most days. I've lost thirty pounds in weight since my heart attack and..."

Tom was interrupted mid-sentence by Dr. Walsh.

"Did you say heart attack? No wonder you're stressed, you should have told me before. Look Tom, anxiety is one of the big symptoms that recovering heart attack patients experience. No wonder you're experiencing memory loss, your body went through one major trauma. You've got to believe me that there are many people out there with much more severe cases of stress induced disorders. No, my advice to you is to try to relax, maybe take up yoga, continue golfing, and enjoy your life." She got up and Rose and Tom knew that they were being dismissed.

"Well, that went well, Tom. Are you feeling any better now that you've passed the test?"

"Oh love, you don't know how relieved I feel. I'm so happy, it's like a huge weight has been lifted off my shoulders."

"Come on then Tom, let's go home and crack open a bottle of wine, we've got some celebrating to do."

THIRTY-ONE

It was not until four o'clock the following day that Ian Green finally got around to phoning Susan. Although she had tried to dismiss her hurt feelings, Susan had spent the day feeling thoroughly depressed and unhappy. Her faith in humanity had been sorely crushed and she still couldn't quite believe that gentle, loving Ian had rejected her so cruelly after their blissful night of love making. Had she frightened him off with their intense love making or was he running scared of commitment like so many other men? It didn't really make any sense and so on top of feeling low she had started to worry. Could Ian have been involved in a car accident? Was he ill? All these questions spun around her head and she was almost at the point of picking up the phone and calling him herself when the phone rang.

"Susan, it's me Ian."

Just the sound of his soft voice made Susan relax immediately, but then her anger took hold of her and she could feel her teeth clench.

"Oh, Ian you've finally deigned to call me, I almost didn't answer. Why, may I ask, did you leave without saying goodbye and why has it taken you so long to get in touch?"

There was a deathly silence on the other end of the line and then Ian finally spoke.

"Believe me Susan, I was going to phone you as soon as I'd got home. I didn't want to wake you so I just left quietly. I always feed the chickens every morning at 6:30 and it was already 7:00 when I left your house. When I got home I found my mother in the hen house lying on the floor. She had apparently gone in to feed the chickens herself and had tripped over the water pail. Oh God, Susan, I thought that she was dead. I called for the ambulance and then spent the rest of the day at the hospital. She's broken her hip and is very badly shaken, but she will survive. I stayed with her all day, they've kept her in for observation. I'm picking her up tomor-row. But here's the thing, Susan, it's given me time to think and I've decided that I'm going to have to get a full-time care giver for Mom. I know that she will refuse to go into a nursing home and it may be down the road that she doesn't have the option, it just depends on her recovery, but what I'm saying is having a caregiver to help Mom will free up my time to be with you."

Susan had listened to Ian with her heart in her mouth. Poor Ian, what an awful time he had experienced and all that time she had been blaming him.

"Oh, Ian, poor you. What a worry and how awful for you to find your mom collapsed on the floor. You must be feeling so guilty and now you've made me feel bad too. Mind you, I loved our night together. When can we do it again?"

"Well, I was hoping that I could come over this evening as

it may be my last chance for a while until I get Mom all settled at home. I've got a bottle of wine and some cheese."

"Right, I'll see you soon then."

Susan put the phone down and let out a big sigh of relief and then she glanced at herself in the hall mirror and got a shock. She looked awful. Her hair was all tangled and she had no make-up on and was wearing her old sweatpants and top. She had been running that morning and hadn't bothered to change. With the speed of lightning Susan ran upstairs and stripped off her clothing and stepped into the shower as she wanted to smell nice for her lover. Shivering with delicious anticipation and with a big smile on her face, Susan stepped into the shower and prepared for the night ahead.

THIRTY-TWO

D CI Hargreaves had just got back to London and was sitting in his office with a Tim Horton's coffee and bagel on his desk waiting for his computer to boot up. He had his phone out because before he did anything else he wanted to transcribe his interview with the Henderson's. He was just about to start when his phone rang. It was DC Manning from Timmins.

"John Hargreaves speaking."

"Have you had time to read the report I sent you this morning? My team and I finished our search of Ms. Grantham's apartment and we found some interesting things which I wanted to discuss with you."

All the while Trevor had been speaking John had been tapping on his keyboard opening his emails and finding the report Trevor had sent. There was an attachment included in the detailed report. John clicked on the attachment and found himself looking at a wall with photographs and maps and arrows connecting pieces together. It looked very much like a police investigation flow chart. He scrolled down and looked at pictures of a framed photograph of David Grantham and then of one showing Maddie and her mother and father. He scrolled back up to the wall and enlarged what looked like a list of names taped to the wall. What he immediately noticed was the yellowing paper and the Queen's University letterhead.

"Trevor, I have the photographs of the living room wall up on my screen and I'm particularly interested in the old piece of paper with the university letterhead. There appear to be twelve names written on it. Can you elaborate at all?"

"Just hang on a minute, John, I'll go and fetch the case box where we put everything after we'd finished photographing the rooms."

John could hear some rustling of papers and then Trevor was back on the phone.

"Here we are, yes, it's a petition signed by twelve women requesting the removal of professor Grantham from the faculty. I see that your friend, Rose Blair's name is on the list although she wasn't a Blair then, her maiden name is Armstrong, Rose Armstrong."

"Is there a Jean and an Eileen on the list?" John asked tentatively.

"Why, yes there is, a Jean Munroe and an Eileen Simpson."

"I have a theory about that list and our Ms. Grantham. Remember I told you that her father had committed suicide after he was fired from the university. This petition was what tipped the scale and forced the faculty to demand his resignation. I know that it sounds a bit far fetched, but I think that Maddie has been seeking vengeance and retribution for what happened to her father all those years ago."

"But why go after the husbands and not the women on that list? I presume that you're talking about those consortiums and the so called accidents'\, that have been bugging you?"

"Well, in answer to your question just think about it. If you wanted to avenge your father's death you would want the person to suffer like her own mother suffered. I'd like to bet that every woman on that list has been widowed in the past eight years."

"Why the past eight years?"

"The consortiums started up in 2012. I think that David Grantham headed up each consortium under different pseudonyms. I'm still checking into this but it's definitely looking that way at the moment. I know for sure that Eileen and Jean were widowed a short while ago and that Rose Blair was targeted to be the next widow. I'll get back to searching for the rest of the names on the list and see how many women have been widowed and how many of their husbands were part of a consortium."

"So, what you're telling me is that this Ms. Grantham deliberately set out to somehow lure the husbands into joining the consortium, fleeced them out of $200,000, and then murdered them in a way that would appear to be an accident. Boy, it still sounds somewhat far-fetched to me."

"The only way that we can prove this is by checking out each name on this list which sounds as if you're already doing that. Now, I wanted to talk to you about David Grantham's murder. The SOC team managed to get a good plaster cast off the tyre print we found at the tailing-pond. It did not match the Lincoln Navigator's tyres but matched, through size and weight, the Audi Quatro driven by the gang members of the Ukrainian mafia we've been watching for years. Olaskiy, Petro, Kateryna, and Ivan have been on our radar and we do know that David Grantham had dealings with them over raising money for the proposed Timmins casino. The most likely scenario is that David got up to his eyes in debt and borrowed substantial amounts of money from the Ukrainians. They probably offed him as an example to other people on their payroll, a gentle warning of what might happen if you don't cough up. We're rounding up the gang and are hauling them into the police station to be interviewed. If we can find the Audi we might find some traces of blood from the scene although I suspect the body was dumped in the back of the Lincoln Navigator and then dumped in the tailing-pond. Anyway, I'm not holding my breath that we'll find anything incriminating, they're as slippery as eels those Ukrainians. I'll let you go now, just keep me up to speed on the consortium murders. It's got me thoroughly intrigued."

John ended the call and sat back at his desk deep in thought. His coffee had gone cold and he no longer had any hunger for the bagel. Right now, his priority was to seek out all the names on the petition and see just how many of the women were now widows.

THIRTY-THREE

Rose and Tom dropped Ben and Puff off with Kate in London and set off on their journey to Kingston. They had decided to stay an extra night at The Holiday Inn as Tom had got it into his head that they would make a little holiday of it, and he really wanted to take Abby and Ella to Fort Henry.

The journey to Kingston was uneventful, the 401 was as busy as ever and the snail's pace through Toronto was exactly as anticipated, but there were no accidents or hold-ups on the road and they made quite good time arriving at their destination one hour before they had arranged to meet Jessica and the girls.

The Holiday Inn was situated right down by the lake on Princess Street. Tom had booked a suite with two queen beds and a small adjoining sitting room. It would be just perfect for them and the big bonus was that there were two swimming pools, one inside and one outside which the girls would love.

Rose bounced on the bed and declared that the room was quite lovely.

"I do fancy a cup of tea though," she said, and Tom laughed.

"We've got a kettle and tea bags and even milk in the fridge. I'll make you a cup, love, if that's what you want and then I'll wander down to the foyer and wait for Jessica and the girls."

"Oh, I do feel as if I'm on holiday, Tom. Just look at the view from our window."

Tom walked over and looked out at the blue waters of Lake Ontario. Somehow the lake looked different from Lake Huron. *I'm probably just imagining it,* Tom thought, but Lake Ontario didn't look nearly as blue as their Lake Huron.

The kettle boiled and Tom made Rose her tea and then he left her relaxing on the sofa with her feet propped up on the coffee table, a contented smile on her face. She knew that this would probably be her last moment of divine peace before Abby and Ella descended upon them with their endless chatter and demands.

Thirty minutes later Rose could hear their chattering down the corridor and suddenly the door burst open and Abby and Ella rushed in followed by Jessica and Tom.

"Grandma, Grandma," the girls shouted in chorus and Rose got up and hugged her darling granddaughters.

"So lovely to see you all again, my darlings." She looked at their daughter Jessica and could see her tired face.

"You'll have a meal with us before you head back to Montreal, won't you darling? You need a bit of a break from driving."

"Yes, I'll have a quick meal, but then I must hit the road

again. I want to be home before it gets dark."

The girls were desperate to go for a swim and so Tom volunteered to go outside and keep an eye on them. Neither Rose or Tom had brought their own bathing suits and so supervising Abby and Ella would be strictly poolside.

As soon as they left the room Jessica said, "Mom, Dad looks better than I've seen him for ages. He's lost that hang-dog expression."

"Well Jess, your father was convinced that he had the beginnings of dementia. He went to the doctor and was referred to The Memory Clinic in Goderich and just yesterday he was tested and passed with flying colours. So now that he realizes that he doesn't actually have dementia he is like a new person and happy again."

Jessica laughed, "Wow Mom, talk about all in the mind. Anyway, I'm happy that he doesn't have dementia, it would have been terribly hard on you."

"Yes, I know, darling, I was really worried about him. Anyway, enough about us old folk, what about you and Rob, how are things going with the two of you?"

Jessica and Rob had moved to Montreal from London three years ago and at first Tom and Rose had felt devastated as they were used to seeing their grandchildren quite regularly and Montreal seemed like a million miles away. The move for Jessica and Rob had been the best thing all round for their marriage and their careers. Rose and Tom saw Abby and Ella three or four times a year and with FaceTime they regularly kept in touch.

"I love Montreal. I can finally say that I'm bilingual as I can actually think in French now and hold a proper conversation in French. Of course Abby and Ella picked up the language almost in their sleep and Rob took FSL lessons paid for by the bank. No, we're happy, just wish that we were nearer to Dad and you."

"Your father and I were thinking about coming up to Quebec in the Fall and visiting you as well as touring the Eastern Townships with all those vineyards. I've been reading the Louise Penny books and have a hankering to source out where Three Pines is supposed to be as I think it's meant to be somewhere in that region."

"That would be great Mom, just tell me when and I'll book some time off work. The girls would love it."

Just then they heard footsteps and laughter and the door burst open to Abby, Ella, and Tom.

"We had such a fab time Grandma, and Grandpa has promised us ice-cream."

Rose smiled and said, "Right you two, get yourselves out of those wet bathing suits and we'll head out in ten minutes. Let's go to Chez-Piggy for a late lunch so that your mom can eat and get back on the road."

Abby and Ella took themselves off to the bedroom to change. Tom sat down and mopped his brow.

"It's pretty hot outside, love. Those two monkeys certainly are nonstop. Where do they get their energy?"

Ten minutes later all five were headed across Princess Street towards the little cobbled alleyway that led to the enchanting restaurant, Chez-Piggy. It was opened in 1979 by Zai Yanosky and Rose Richardson, both members of the sixties pop group, The Lovin Spoonfuls. An old limestone stable built in 1806 set in a small courtyard tucked behind a large, impressive building had been converted into the restaurant. As they walked down the narrow alley Abby and Ella speculated what they would find. Abby was convinced the place would be haunted, but Ella said that it more likely would be like an animal farm with pigs in the courtyard. Of course, it was none of these, the actual restaurant was quite sophisticated, although Rose remembered visiting Chez-Piggy in the nineties and it had a far more rustic, almost hippie feel to it then. There were round tables out on the patio sheltered by colourful umbrellas and Tom suggested that they sit outside.

"This is lovely, Mom and Dad. Didn't you bring all of us here as a family years ago? It hasn't changed much, has it?"

"Yes, you were only a little girl and Paul was a toddler. Your father and I have been back here several times since, but it pretty well has stayed the same. I just love the fact that it's hidden down an alleyway, it's got such a European vibe, like being in old Quebec City."

They ordered their meals and chatted away amicably and then Abby reminded Tom that he had promised them ice-cream. Rose had spotted an ice-cream vendor down by the marina close to the hotel.

"I tell you what, girls, we'll walk your mom back to the car, say our goodbyes and then we'll go and get your ice-creams. Okay?"

Jessica nodded her approval as she was anxious to get back on the road. She had a good four hour journey ahead of her and she hated driving in the dark, particularly on the 401.

Waving goodbye to their mother Abby and Ella stood next to Tom and Rose watching Jessica drive away.

"Right, I scream, you scream, we all scream for ice-cream." Tom sang out and the girls clapped their hands and squealed with delight.

"Come on then, let's go and get an ice-cream."

THIRTY-FOUR

The following morning, sitting around the breakfast table in what was called The Orangery, Tom, Rose, Abby, and Ella ate their buffet-style breakfast with relish. They had forgone supper the previous night as all four of them were still full from their late lunch and ice-cream, but now, fifteen hours later, they were ravenous.

"Now, I've planned a trip to Fort Henry for today and then Grandma wants to show you the university that she attended. We thought that a swim in between the Fort visit and the university would probably be in order. So, eat up and we'll get going."

Fort Henry was situated on a high bluff overlooking the mouth of the Cataraqui River where it flowed into the St. Lawrence at the east end of Lake Ontario. The Fort had been built by the British military in 1812 and was very largely still intact.

They parked the car in a massive carpark and were shuttled to the Fort where they were immediately greeted by

soldiers dressed in red uniforms. There were soldiers everywhere and in the large parade ground the soldiers practised
their drill. Around the perimeter of the Fort there were a
number of enclosed rooms. Rose and Tom ushered the girls
into one such room – a school room. The teacher was a very
stern looking woman dressed in a plain cotton long sleeved
dress and bonnet. Immediately as Abby and Ella entered she
commanded the girls to sit on one side of the classroom, boys
were on the other side. They were given a slate and a piece of
chalk to write on.

"Straight backs, eyes to the front, feet together and no talking," and so the lesson began. Tom and Rose stood at the back
of the room and watched as the children were put through
their paces. When they were finished, Abby and Ella both said
that they were so pleased that they didn't live in those times.

They visited the blacksmiths shop and watched horseshoes
being beaten into shape and then they went to the 'tuck' shop
and were given little cornets filled with hard candy.

Tom looked at his watch and then at Rose who appeared to
be flagging. The trouble was the heat and very little shade. He
decided it was time the whole family headed back to the hotel.

Rose kicked her shoes off and went to lie down. Their
hotel room was blissfully cool after the heat of the day, where
even Abby and Ella looked exhausted.

"We'll just rest up for a bit." Tom said, "Maybe you girls
might like to watch some television while Grandma and
Grandpa lie down? I'll take you to the swimming pool afterwards, okay?"

The girls eagerly agreed and sat down on the sofa and
began to cable-surf. Tom left them to it and climbed onto the
bed next to Rose and soon was snoring gently while she read

her book. The girls appeared to be immersed in whatever it was they watching.

Half an hour later Abby crept into the bedroom and asked when they were going to the swimming pool. Rose looked at Tom sound asleep and decided that it was her turn to supervise the girls. She got off the bed and padded quietly into the sitting room.

"Okay, time to get your bathers on. Grab a couple of towels and let's get going to the pool. We'll leave Grandpa here in peace."

Forty minutes later Rose was once again sweaty and hot. There was little shade around the outdoor pool. She finally called the girls out of the water and proceeded to walk back to their hotel room. Tom was awake and watching golf on the television.

"Wow, it's so hot out there, Tom. Look, it's almost five I think that we should find somewhere to eat and then we can spend the evening driving around the university campus. I'd also like to try and find my old digs."

"What are digs, Grandma?" Ella asked.

"Digs are where people live, mostly students and they often share a house with other students just like I did."

"Who did you share with, Grandma?" Ella seemed interested in the idea of digs.

"Let me see, there was Pia Sarchelli."

"Pia, that's a funny name."

Tom piped up, "Yes, she was one hot Italian girl, quite stunning."

"Tom, fancy you remembering her. Yes, well, all the men on the campus fancied Pia."

It was then that Rose remembered that Pia was one of the

student's who had signed the petition to oust out Professor Grantham, she had been one of the most vociferous of the students to strike out against the professor.

Tom piped up again, "I think that she ended up marrying one of my mates, Russell Wilson, you remember him, Rose, tall chap with a mop of blond hair."

Rose vaguely remembered Pia dating a good-looking chap, but that last year at university was still such a blur to her as Tom and she were dating and so wrapped up in each other they were barely aware of anything or anyone else.

"Right, so where shall we go for dinner?"

Abby and Ella both shouted together, "McDonald's!"

Rose looked at Tom and they both rolled their eyes and then laughed.

"Okay, McDonald's it is, are you both ready? Tom can you source out the nearest McDonald's or do you want me to? I'm not sure where I've put my phone, though."

Tom pulled out his phone and Googled in the name of the restaurant.

"Here, I've got it, the closest one is on 285 Princess Street actually not too far from here. It's probably only about four blocks away so we could easily walk. Princess Street is one way so driving there we would have to go down Brock. Let's just walk, it's a lovely evening."

"Okay, off we go, are you girls ready?"

Abby and Ella had been squabbling about who got to choose the television program and it sounded as if Ella was winning when Rose called out to them.

Finally, they set off down Princess Street and within fifteen minutes they had reached McDonald's and soon were devouring some Big Macs and fries. Rose could not remember the last time they had eaten at McDonald's and one thing for certain was that the coffee had vastly improved in taste since then. Their meal was consumed within twenty minutes, *hence the term fast food*, Rose thought wryly. On their way back to the hotel they stopped off at a Dollarama and Tom gave the girls five dollars each to spend on whatever they fancied. While they shopped, Rose picked up some chocolates for that evening and some snacks for their return journey the next day. They arrived back at the hotel twenty minutes later and Rose suggested that they hopped in the car and went for a drive around the campus before settling down for the evening at The Holiday Inn.

Queen's University was about two kilometres away driving up Brock Street, turning left at Bagot, just past the library and through the city park, passing the cricket field brought them out by the University School of Medicine on Barry Street.

Ella asked Rose, "So Grandma, where are your digs?"

"Oh, darling, I lived somewhere off Kensington Avenue, I can't remember exactly where but I know it was within walking distance of my faculty."

Tom replied, "I've just remembered who your third flat-mate was, love, it was Angela Watson and she married Tony Bright, you know that whiz-kid. He went on to be a CFO of one of the major Canadian Banks. I remember reading about him in the Financial Times last year. Talking of which, do remind me to pick up a newspaper from the lobby when we get back to the hotel, love."

They turned into the main campus and Rose pointed out the English Department and the Arts Centre which used to house the theatre. Most of the university campus had not changed much until they got to a whole section of very new looking buildings which were student hall of residences.

"Now these are all new, Tom. I wouldn't have minded living here in the day."

"Are these your digs, Grandma?" Ella asked from the back seat of their car.

"Oh no, darling, these are far too fancy and new. I lived in an old house with peeling paint and wonky floors."

Rose remembered the house well now that they were on the campus. It had been a really run-down student let, probably built in the 1920's. The landlady lived in the basement flat and was very strict about the comings and goings on at the house. Strictly no parties were allowed, and she frowned upon male visitors. But Angela, Pia, and Rose had all got on well together and the atmosphere inside the run down, messy house was always sweet and harmonious.

"Seen enough, love?" Tom asked. "Shall we head back to the hotel now?"

"Yes Tom, let's go back before I get too nostalgic for years gone by."

Back at the hotel they found a suitable family movie for all of them to watch together. Rose brought out the chocolates and they settled into a comfortable evening.

Later in bed that night, Tom pulled out the newspaper he had bought up from the lobby. Rose was reading her book when Tom let out a gasp.

"Good God," he said, "I've just been reading the Toronto Stock Exchange and would you believe it my Silvercorp shares have increased in value by three hundred percent. Maybe I should be selling them."

THIRTY-FIVE

J ohn Hargreaves had begun the onerous task of trying
to track down every name on the Queens University
petition dated 1973. In order to find the spouses of
the women on the list he had to search the Provincial
Registry for births, deaths, and marriages and this indeed was
a bit like looking for a needle in a haystack. He was just
thinking about delegating the task when a thought
struck him.

Bloody hell, he thought, *what was I thinking.* Well he had
not been thinking clearly as John trolled back through his
communications with Trevor Manning from Timmins. He
finally found the photographs from Maddie Grantham's living
room wall. This was the centre, the hub of her investigation
and this was where John was convinced he would find all of
the names of the spouses on the petition, after all, she would
have had to have searched them out for herself. Sure enough,
as he traced the arrows on the wall he found a list of men's
names connecting up to the women's names on the list.

Maddie had certainly done her research and it was now all there for him to follow.

Soon John had the completed list of twelve women and their husbands. He would now have to research the death certifications issued by the Province of Ontario and gain access to the medical certificates of cause of death records in order to establish how the men had died. By the end of the day he had fully completed the list and was shocked by the array of different accidental deaths. There had been cycling accidents, hit-and-run, sailing accidents, falling down a flight of stairs, two questionable heart attacks, one fall from a ladder, one death from cancer, another car accident involving brake failure, and finally a climbing accident. There had been no police investigations involved in any of the deaths.

John clicked off his computer and sat at his desk once again deep in thought. It would be one hell of a job trying to get a murder rap on all or indeed any of the accidental deaths. So far, the attempted murder of Tom Blair held the strongest case for conviction. They would have to wait and see if and when Ms. Grantham made a recovery. In the meantime, he would try to put together a cohesive report on what he called the consortium murders.

DC Trevor Manning let out an exasperated sigh. He had just heard that the police had found a thoroughly torched Audi Quattro out on one of the county side roads. Gone now was any possible evidence of David Grantham's murder.

The interview with Olasky, Petro, Kateryna, and Ivan had also proved to be a sorry affair. The men all had solid alibis for the time of death of the victim and, indeed, all four of them denied all knowledge of even knowing the man. There had been no witnesses. It looked like the case would end up in the cold-case files and maybe, just maybe, down the road, the Ukrainian gang might slip up and they would be able to cross-reference and open the case again. Trevor sighed again. It was always extremely frustrating when a case went cold. On the other hand, he wondered how DCI John Hargreaves had faired with the consortium case. He picked up the phone and called John.

"John Hargreaves speaking."

"Oh, hi John, it's Trevor. I just thought I'd let you know that we interviewed the Ukrainian gang and unfortunately they all clammed-up like oysters. Tight alibis too, so it looks like it's going to be filed away as an unresolved murder. How about you? What's been happening with your consortium scams?"

John paused before he spoke. "Yes, well I've pretty well proven my hypothesis that the husbands in the consortiums were being systematically bumped off leaving the women who signed the petition, all widows. I suppose it was done as a form of retribution for the suffering inflicted upon her mother. However, to get a conviction, the so-called accidental deaths would have to be ruled out and replaced with solid proof of murder by intent and I doubt very much that is going to happen. The best I can work with right now is the attempted murder on Tom Blair and even that is going to be hard getting a conviction. You know it was a very clever plan, expertly enacted and born of many years of planning. Should our Ms. Grantham recover I know that she'll deny all part in the execution of the plan. After all she is a lawyer herself. It's all very frustrating. I intend to visit the hospital again tomorrow and see if there's any improvement. Changing the subject, how did your date with the lovely Susan Parker go?"

Trevor was quiet. He had replayed the whole bizarre evening in his mind time and time again and still had come up feeling somewhat confused.

"Oh, we had a lovely dinner catching up on old times. The chemistry between us seemed to still be there and I thought that we were getting along famously and then she got a text message, and it was as if she switched courses after that. I really like her though and I was sort of led to believe that she was free. Mind you, I also think that it's still too soon for me to be even thinking about any relationships. My divorce was particularly acrimonious. Oh well, it's back to online dating for me, but thanks for asking."

They ended the call and both men sat back at their respective desks deep in thought. Life sometimes threw out a curve ball which was supposed to be challenging and life changing but neither of the men particularly welcomed the challenge.

THIRTY-SIX

The journey back to Bayfield seemed to fly by probably because Abby and Ella never stopped talking. The snacks that Rose had bought were devoured within the first hour and they were forced to stop for several pee breaks, but other than that good time was made, and they were back in the village by mid-afternoon. Tom and Rose had decided to leave the dogs at Kate and John's and pick them up the next day when they were going to London for John's surprise birthday party. Rose could tell that Kate would have far preferred them to have swung by and got the dogs before the party, but for once Rose stuck to her guns and didn't capitulate.

Of course the minute Abby and Ella entered their house they wanted to know where Puff and Ben were and why were they staying with Aunty Kate and who was John? So many questions, it quite exhausted Rose. She suggested that Tom might take the girls to the beach while she prepared dinner as a bit of peace and quiet was what Rose really craved. She opened the fridge to see what she could find to make for their dinner. There was a packet of sausages; she would make toad-in-the-hole, one of Tom's favourite dishes. Peeling the potatoes, chopping the carrots, and frying the sausages soon destressed Rose. It was always amazing how the simple task of cooking could be like balm to her soul. Rose whipped up the batter for the toad-in-the-hole, lay the sausages in an oven proof dish, poured some of the sizzling fat over them, and then added the batter. Putting the whole lot in the hot oven, Rose turned the vegetables on to cook and then went to lay the table. They would have ice-cream and chocolate sauce for dessert as she didn't feel like making a pudding.

The phone rang just as Rose was about to sit down and read a book. It was her friend Susan.

"Oh hi, Susan. I haven't spoken to you for ages. How is everything?"

"Well, I've got tons to tell you. Are you going to be around for a bit, can I come over?"

Rose paused, "Well, we've got Abby and Ella here right now, Tom's taken them to the beach and then we'll have supper. Maybe later, around 7:00 when I've got the girls settled you could pop over for a glass of wine and then you can fill me in with all your news."

With that agreed upon Rose put the phone down, checked the toad, and then went back to the sofa to snatch another ten minutes of peace to herself.

Tom returned with the girls twenty minutes later. Their faces were flushed and glowing with the sun and fresh air.

"We wanted to swim but we didn't have our bathing suits." Abby complained. "Grandpa said he would take us to the beach tomorrow for a proper swim."

"Yes, we'll all go to the beach in the morning, but we've got the party at Aunty Kate's house in London in the afternoon."

"Are we getting Puff and Ben then?" Ella asked plaintively. "I miss them so much."

"Yes, darling, we'll bring the dogs back here and Aunty Kate has a cat now, he's called Miffy."

Rose could see by their excited faces that having a cat to play with would be the highlight of their trip to London.

"Okay, I've got to make the gravy and then we'll sit up for dinner. Now go and wash your hands both of you."

Five minutes later they were sitting around the table with plates of toad-in-the-hole in front of them.

"You girls have eaten toad-in-the-hole before, haven't you?" Rose asked after watching Abby pick at her food in a fussy way.

"Yuk, we're eating toads, are we?" Ella said as she threw her fork down on the table.

"Silly girl, toad-in-the-hole is just sausages in a batter, a bit like Yorkshire pudding. It's Grandpa's favourite meal, isn't it Grandpa?"

Tom was half-way through eating his meal and nodded appreciatively at Rose.

"Sure is my favourite right next to Shepherd's Pie. Come on you two, just try it and see."

Abby and Ella tentatively took a mouthful, then another, and soon they were tucking into their meal with gusto. The fresh lake air had made them hungry.

"Susan's coming over later, Tom." Rose said.

"Oh yes, does she know that we've got the girls here?" Tom said while eyeing up the leftovers sitting on the work top.

"Would you like some more, Tom? Oh, and yes she does

know the girls are here. They can watch television while we sit in the kitchen and catch up."

"Well, I might just pop down to The Albion for a pint while you two gossip."

Half an hour later Abby and Ella were sitting in front of the television engrossed in watching the musical, "Annie." Tom had gone to The Albion and Rose had just cleaned the kitchen when the front doorbell rang. It was Susan. Rose let her in.

"Wow, it's so quiet without the dogs barking." Susan said.

"Yes, it does seem strange without the dogs racing to the front door. Anyway, come in and go through to the kitchen. Tom's gone for a drink and the girls are watching a movie. I was about to microwave some popcorn for them. You could open the wine while I deal with the popcorn and then we can relax."

With that done Susan and Rose sat down at the kitchen table and both eagerly drank their glass of wine. Rose went first.

"So, tell me all about your date with Trevor?"

Susan looked blank, "Oh, you know Rose I'd completely forgotten all about that, nothing happened. I chickened out in the end after Ian texted me and I suddenly felt awfully guilty as if I was betraying him having dinner with Trevor. I'm afraid I let him down big time."

Rose looked surprised as she was expecting to hear that they had spent the night together. Maybe, just maybe, Ian Green might prove to be the right man for her friend.

"You know Ian and I hadn't really gone past first base, other than a bit of kissing and I was beginning to wonder when he would make a move. Well, he finally did, and we've spent the night together although that's a whole different story, and he came over again last night. Oh, Rose, I think that I'm in love."

Rose looked at her friend and she could immediately see that Susan had that particular glow of someone in the first flush of love. Maybe it was just the sex, but whatever it was her friend looked positively radiant.

"Well, changing the subject somewhat," Rose said, "You know we were in Kingston, and I visited the university which, by the way, hasn't changed that much, but while I was there Tom remembered that my housemates were also drama students who had signed that petition. Pia Sarchelli and Angela Watson. Pia married Russel Wilson who died a couple of years ago in a boating accident, and Angela married Tony Bright who became CFO of some Canadian bank, now I don't know if he's still alive."

"Gosh, so our theory seems to be panning out." Susan said. "Difficult to prove though even if it all looks suitably fishy unless the deaths were considered suspect at the time. The consortium connection could form a case, but my gut feeling is that it would be extremely difficult to get any conviction without a police case being opened up."

"We'll be in London at Kate and John's house tomorrow; I'll ask John what he thinks. Have you heard if Maddie is still in intensive care?"

"I haven't heard or seen anyone, but you could probably find that out tomorrow. I have a horrible feeling that this whole case will end up being one of those unresolved cases. We'll have to wait and see what Serious Crimes has come up with."

"Oh, I almost forgot, Tom passed his memory test with

flying colours and he's like a new man now that he doesn't think he's got dementia."

"Well, that as well as having the stress of someone attempting to kill him taken away, no wonder the man feels so happy. Poor Tom, what a weight off his shoulders."

"So, Susan, what happens next with Ian? Do you think that you might move in with each other?

Susan looked pensive. "The trouble is Rose, his mother. She's in her nineties and still lives at home and Ian feels a strong sense of filial duty to look after his mom. She took a fall so he's arranged for One-Care to visit, but to be honest she probably needs to be in a home. Ian won't hear of it so we don't talk about that. I guess I'll just have to get used to him not spending the night with me."

"What about cooking, does his mom manage to cook?"

"Well before her fall she was fully independent; in fact, she always had a hot dinner waiting for Ian when he came home from work. But now she's not so mobile so Ian has got Meals-on-Wheels delivering her lunch and then he rushes home from work and cook's dinner, settles her in for the night, and then comes over to my house."

"Does his mom know that he's seeing someone?"

"I honestly don't know, Rose, but I do think that Ian needs to tell her. Maybe I should visit her myself, what do you think?"

"It probably would be better if Ian prepares the way first and that he's with you when you visit. But yes, if you think that your feelings for Ian are real then it probably is about time that you met his mother."

Just then Abby and Ella came running in. "Grandma, can we have some milk and cookies, please?"

"Yes, of course darlings, I'll bring some in for you both. Say hallo to my friend Susan, I'm sure that you've met before."

"Hi," Abby and Ella said and skipped out of the kitchen and back to watching the rest of "Annie."

"They're both so cute," Susan said, "How long are they staying here with you?"

"They're here for a week. Tomorrow will be taken up with going to London and then on Sunday we are planning to take them to Grand Bend for the day."

Susan pulled a face. "It will be like hell with the lid off," she said and Rose knew exactly what she was saying, but Tom had insisted that a Grand Bend visit and beach day was an essential part of any holiday. Bayfield beach was nice, but Grand Bend beach was spectacular.

"Well, if you're desperate to escape just give me a call. Oh, and let me know how it all goes with John tomorrow." Susan said as she got up to leave. She poked her head around the corner of the living room and said goodbye to the girls.

After Susan had left, Rose poured herself out the last of the bottle of wine and sat in the kitchen just savouring the silence.

THIRTY-SEVEN

John reached the hospital by nine that following morning. He had promised Kate to be in London no later than twelve as it was his birthday and she had said that a restaurant had been booked for mid-day. As he walked into the intensive care unit, he heard a loud commotion. Nurses and doctors were running, one with a cardiac defibrillator on a trolley and he could hear an urgent voice giving out instructions. He soon realized that it was what he had suspected, Maddie Grantham, who, by the looks of things, had gone into cardiac arrest.

"Stand back," the doctor commanded as the paddles were placed on Maddie's chest. John watched her body as it arched with the electric currents passing through. He shook his head and was suddenly enveloped in a cloak of sadness. He should not have been witnessing this largely personal ordeal, it seemed somehow unethical and wrong. John slipped away and went to sit in the small waiting room at the entrance way to the IC unit.

Twenty minutes later a young nurse appeared and asked if she could help him.

"DCI Hargreaves," John said, "I came to see Ms. Grantham, but I could see that there was an emergency going on when I arrived. How is she?"

The nurse looked awkward. "I'm afraid to tell you that she didn't make it; Ms Grantham is dead."

John felt shocked to hear that Maddie Grantham had died. He somehow had thought that she would pull through, he honestly thought that she would live to fight the case brought against her.

He got up to leave but was met at the door by the doctor he recognized from the resuscitation team.

"I'm Dr. Parker, I saw you come into Ms. Grantham's room. I gather that you've already been told that she didn't make it and I really think that it is for the best. Had she come out of the coma she might have been severely brain damaged. It will be hard on her parents. Please give them our condolences."

Yes, it will be hard particularly for Sylvia as she had so recently lost her brother-in-law and now her daughter, John thought as he got into his car and drove back to London.

THIRTY-EIGHT

The guests had all been instructed to arrive around twelve. Kate had invited just a small gathering of mostly family and close friends. The trouble with both John and she being relative newcomers to the area they did not have many friends or, for that matter, family. John's only daughter, Rachel, her husband, and their child were his only family living in Canada and Rose and Tom were Kate's only family in Ontario. Her daughter was in New Zealand and her other children still lived back in Kelowna, B.C. close to their father, her ex. She had invited a couple of friends from Bayfield and a couple from her present job at Labatt's. There would be twelve people which was a nice number to cater. Kate had truly cooked up a storm, mostly finger foods, but she had made a large sea-food paella, one of John's favourite dishes and a large lasagne. The only thing she did not make herself was the birthday cake and that she had bought from the supermarket.

Across the entrance hallway Kate had strung a birthday banner and she had also gone to town with balloons everywhere. If nothing else the children could take them home to play with, Miffy was certainly enjoying chasing them across the room.

John arrived back home just after 11:30. He had stopped for a coffee in Lucan and now, under strict orders from Kate, was upstairs showering and changing into some decent clothes for their lunch date. She had suggested to the party guests that they hide their cars from view, Kate was really wanting to make the party a big surprise. John, however, had caught on the minute that he had returned home. He had chuckled to himself but decided to go along with the charade and pretend that it was all a huge surprise.

Everyone came into the house and Kate, with her finger to her mouth, herded everyone into the dining room and closed the door. They could hear John talking to Kate and then as she opened the dining-room door they all shouted "Surprise!" on top of their voices. The party began, champagne was served, music played, and Ben and Puff were let into the house and were ecstatic to see Rose and Tom. Abby and Ella disappeared off with Miffy and everyone appeared to be having a great time.

Finally, Rose managed to corner John. Despite her reservations Rose steeled herself to be strong, she would not let the man get to her. Her resolution lasted all of three minutes and then she felt her heart beat faster and her body begin to yearn for his touch.

"John, can I ask you how the attempted murder case is coming on?"

John looked at Rose and she could immediately tell that he too was feeling the electric current between them. He licked his lips and shook his head and then began in a whisper to talk to Rose.

"Rose, you have bewitched me again, I can barely breathe. I so want to take you to my room and devour every inch of your body."

Rose looked around the room nervously. Kate was engrossed in a conversation with Rachel and her husband, Tom was out in the garden with Abby, Ella, and the dogs, and the other guests all seemed preoccupied. She turned to John.

"We're just being daft, John. In another life you and I could have had amazing sex, but not this one. I love Tom and that's the end of it. Now, you never answered my question about the investigation?"

"Scarlet woman, you," John laughed, and the tension was broken. "Actually, I've got some sad news to tell you and Tom. Maddie Grantham just died this morning of cardiac arrest."

"Oh, gosh, John, that's awful, poor Sylvia and Brian. Well, I suppose that closes the case, at least you won't have to deal with a legal battle. I must tell Tom, I'm sure that he'll be equally as sad. You know, I think that he had a little crush on her."

Rose left John feeling very low in spirits. Her heart went out to Sylvia and Brian as no parents should ever have to see their children go before them. On the bright side though, with Maddie gone Tom could really put the whole consortium to rest. All he had to do now was to sell his shares.

Kate rounded everyone up for the lighting of the cake and they all sang "Happy Birthday" to John with gusto. The party began to wind down and so did Tom and Rose. At least she wouldn't have to cook that night, Rose thought as they called Abby and Ella to say goodbye to their aunt. Tom fetched the dogs and Kate and Rose hugged each other promising to be in touch. It was the end of a lovely party and Rose was ready to go home.

The rest of Abby and Ella's visit whizzed by at a rate of knots and soon it was time for their parents to pick them up. Jessica and Rob had wanted to spend the weekend in Bayfield and so, for two days, Rose felt that she had done nothing but cook and make endless pots of coffee. It was always lovely to see the family, but equally nice to see them leave.

Finally, the house was back to normal, Tom returned to his games of golf and Rose caught up with her friends. One evening, a few weeks later, Rose asked Tom if he had sold his shares. Tom frowned. "I went to see my friend the lawyer. I wanted him to make a codicil to the shareholders agreement saying that if anything should happen to me you will inherit my shares because, you see, love, the way it's set up right now if I should die the shares would automatically go back to Silver-corp and we don't want that, do we. My buddy reminded me that should I want to sell my shares then Silvercorp has to be given first option to buy. He suggested that I might approach one of the other silver mines up in that area and see if they might be interested in purchasing the shares."

Rose looked doubtful, "Just be careful, Tom. You'll have to talk to Brian before you do anything else. What are the shares worth now on the stock exchange?"

Tom disappeared off to his study and Rose could hear him clicking away on the keyboard. Then he heard him exclaim,

"Good God, they've gone up even more, they are now four times what I paid for them."

Rose did the maths and then again. If Tom was now the sole consortium member the $800,000 had now multiplied to 3.2 million. Over three million dollars, that was unbelievable.

"Tom, you do realize that if you sell those shares we stand to be very, very rich. What we will need to do is to give Jean and Eileen their $200,000 back and then heaven only knows what we'll do with the rest. I think that you should get in touch with Brian Henderson and offer him first dibs of the shares."

"Yes, I know, love. I wanted to give the Henderson's time to mourn their daughter before I approached him, but I will contact Brian soon and get the ball moving."

"Well, the sooner the better. I want all your connections to Silvercorp severed. It makes me feel uncomfortable, everything about it."

"Yes, I agree, love, but don't forget the money. Alex, I mean David, always said that we would make a big profit and a large return on out investment and he was quite right."

"Okay, well, maybe at the Croquet Club cocktail party you might be able to talk to Brian casually and feel the water's so to speak."

"Right, I'll do that, love, isn't it the cocktail party tomorrow?"

"Yes, and we're supposed to be helping to host. I'm making a large lasagne and bringing a couple of baguettes; Melissa wanted an Italian theme, Marcia's making a huge Caesar salad and Margo's in charge of cookies and squares."

Tom looked at Rose, "Wow, the three M's in action, Margo, Marcia, and Melissa. How come you got involved?"

"Oh, I just offered to help. I don't mind, you know I love cooking."

The next day Rose spent the morning making a very large lasagne. She left it out to cool. She would bring it around to Melissa's before heading out to the croquet courts. They wouldn't need her help setting up, the three M's would manage perfectly well without her.

Tom went off to play golf with Doug promising to be at the cocktail party by five. Rose went off to play croquet and was pleased to see Sylvia and Brian on the courts. They hadn't been out playing croquet that past month, understandably as they had been in deep mourning for the loss of their daughter. Sylvia would never recover from the loss, but time would soften the pain and getting out and about was probably the best way to start the healing process.

Two hours later Rose was at Melissa's house. She carried the hot lasagne out from the oven to the back yard where a long table had been set up complete with a pretty checked tablecloth and matching serviettes. There was a huge cool box filled with ice waiting to receive the guest's bottles of wine and little bowls of olives and almonds sat on tables dotted around the garden.

Rose spotted Sylvia sitting in the shade under a large maple tree. She walked over and seeing a vacant chair pulled it over.

"Hi, Sylvia, how have you been doing?"

"Oh, it's you, Rose. Thank you so much for the lovely flowers and card, it was so thoughtful of you."

"You know where I am, Sylvia, if you ever need to talk to someone please don't hesitate."

Sylvia looked as if she might cry and so Rose got up and

gave her a big hug and then squeezed her hand. "I'm truly sorry for your loss, Sylvia."

She left Sylvia to compose herself and went to find Tom. Rose had noticed Brian standing by the food table and she really wanted Tom to speak to him. *I suppose I could engage him in a conversation*, Rose thought as she looked around for Tom.

"Hi, Brian, I just wanted to say how sorry we are for your tragic loss."

Brian looked at Rose coldly. "If it wasn't for your husband, she would still be alive."

Rose didn't know quite what to say as she didn't want to get into an argument. She was about to walk away when Tom appeared at her side.

"I'll leave you two men to talk," Rose said.

"Brian," Tom said. "I want to talk to you about my Silvercorp shares. Apparently, I must offer them to you to buy first before trading on the stock exchange. I see that they have gone up four times in value."

Brian clapped Tom on his back.

"You've done the right thing coming to me first, but I was going to contact you anyway. You must realize now that you are one of Silvercorp's major shareholders and as such I wanted to invite you to the Annual North Ontario Mining Conference. We've got some exciting news to tell our investors."

"All I want is to sell my shares. I don't want to get involved in conferences and stuff. I just want to be rid of the consortium and all that it has represented."

Tom realized that he had raised his voice and several

people were looking their way. He lowered his tone and once more beseeched Brian to listen.

"Look, I've been in touch with the Red-Deer Mining Company and I believe that they are your main competitors. I offered to sell my shares to them if you refuse to buy them from me. I'm sorry, Brian, I don't wish to cause problems, but I truly do want to sell and soon."

Brian's face clouded over at the mention of the Red Deer Silver Mine. Tom had done his research and it was in the public domain and common knowledge that the two mines were rivals. The big rumour going around was talk of a merger; Silvercorp was looking to buy out Red Deer, however if they were to buy Tom's shares the merger might favour Red Deer buying Silvercorp. Whatever, Tom's meddling would not do Silvercorp any favours.

"Hold your horses, Tom." Brian said, "We can discuss your shares at the conference. Look, I'm flying up to Timmins on Monday and will be back in London by the evening. I promise that what you hear at the conference will really excite you."

Tom could see that he was at an impasse. It might be that he would have to go to the conference if only to placate the man.

"I'll think about it, Brian and let you know tomorrow if I can make it on Monday."

That night Rose and Tom had a big argument. She was dead set against Tom going up to Timmins with Brian Henderson. "I don't trust that man," she said. "He's a blatant liar."

"But love, if I want to be rid of these shares I might just have to go to the conference, besides, Red-Deer Mining company will be there, and it would give me the opportunity to talk to them in person. Look, it's just one day, it might even be quite interesting."

"Well, I suppose it will be alright, but Tom, you have to promise me not to do anything rash. I'm not at all happy at the thought of you in Brian Henderson's clutches."

Tom kissed Rose gently and said, "Don't you worry, love, I'll be just fine, you'll see."

THIRTY-NINE

That Monday Tom decided to drive by himself to London airport as he had declined a ride with Brian on the basis that he was hoping to visit Paul and Atsuko on his return.

One hour later they were airborne aboard a six-seater Piper. There were four other passengers and by the looks of things they were also heading to The Northern Ontario Miners Conference. They all appeared to know Brian and an amicable forty-five minutes passed quickly with plenty of laughter and conviviality. They descended to Timmins Airport at eleven. Brian had rented a car which he drove to The Hilton Conference Centre in downtown Timmins. There were dozens of people, mostly men, Tom observed, lining up to go into the conference which appeared to be handled very efficiently by the staff. Registration tables with pens to write their names to be inserted into lanyards to be worn around the neck and forms to be filled in, Tom had attended enough conferences in his lifetime to know the whole procedure well. Attendees were shown into a large auditorium holding over two hundred people.

Tom looked at the agenda and was shocked to see that the conference spanned two days. How was it that Brian had said that that they would be home that same afternoon? He looked around to find Brian who was chatting earnestly to a couple of men standing by the adjacent table. He overheard some snippets of their conversation and realized that Brian was talking about the merger with the Red-Deer Mining company. He, himself, was anxious to talk to them and so he walked over to the men. Brian scowled at him, but politely made the introductions.

"Tom, meet Gerald White and Jawal Podilinsky. They are our chief competitors in the mining business."

Gerald and Jawal shook Tom's hand and asked if he worked for Silvercorp. Before Tom could answer for himself Brian interrupted him. "Oh, no, Tom is one of our biggest shareholders. I'm trying to entice him to sit on our Board."

The two men immediately showed an interest in Tom and handed him their business cards. When Brian's back was turned, Tom seized the opportunity to say, "I would love to talk to you about my shares. Maybe later we can have a word?"

"Yes, sure, we break for lunch at 12:30, we can get together then."

The conference started and Tom steeled himself to be bored out of his brains, but contrary to his expectations, he found some of the guest speakers quite riveting. By lunch time he felt that his understanding of mining in Ontario had greatly increased.

As soon as Tom had departed Rose felt restless and

extremely agitated. She just had such a bad feeling about Brian Henderson. Picking up her phone she called Susan.

"HI, Susan, can I pop over for a chat or you could come here? I need to talk to you about Tom."

Susan, who had just got out of bed and was half asleep, not being much of a morning person, recognized the worry in Rose's voice.

"Yes, come around but you have to take me as you find me. I'll put the kettle on."

Placing her phone down, Susan dashed upstairs and quickly threw on some clothes, brushed her hair and cleaned her teeth. The doorbell rang just as she had finished washing her face.

"Come in, Rose, I've put the kettle on, coffee or tea?"

"Oh, coffee please."

"We'll sit out on the patio." Susan said as she carried two mugs of steaming coffee outside to the patio.

The courtyard was rather predominated by a huge hot tub, Susan's pride and joy, but there was a pretty circular wrought iron table and two chairs to one side by the fence. Rose and Susan sat down bathed in the early morning sun.

Never one to hold back, Susan dived straight in.

"So, what's the problem?"

"Tom's gone up to Timmins with Brian Henderson and I'm worried sick that something awful is going to happen to him."

Susan could see that her friend was close to tears. *Why on earth would Tom go anywhere near Silvercorp again,* she wondered.

"So, tell me, why did he go back to Timmins?"

"Brian invited him to the Northern Ontario Miners

Conference. It's all because Tom asked Brian if Silvercorp would like first option to buy his shares, you see Tom is considered to be a major shareholder now. Apparently Tom thinks that Silvercorp is in the middle of a merger with their rival mining company Red-Deer, so you see his shares are now a hot commodity. The trouble is, Susan, I really don't trust Brian Henderson. He's up to no good, I just know it."

"Would you like me to speak to my friend Trevor, Sergeant Manning? He might be able to keep an eye on Tom and Brian, although I'm sure Tom will be quite safe while he's at the conference, it's what happens after I would be concerned about."

Rose went quiet while she thought about the implications of what could happen to Tom after the conference.

"If you could talk to Trevor, I would be really grateful. I just have this horrible feeling that something is not right, and that Tom is walking into danger."

"Okay, you drink up your coffee while I make that phone call. Look, everything will be alright just try not to worry."

Susan went inside to fetch her phone, as she tapped in Trevor's number she had pause for thought. Her behaviour on their date had been unforgivable and now she felt thoroughly ashamed of herself. It was time to eat humble-pie and try to make amends.

"Sergeant Manning speaking."

"Hi, Trevor, it's Susan Parker. Look, I really must apologize for my behaviour when we had dinner. I wasn't good company, and you didn't deserve my brush off. With that said, I have a small favour to ask of you...."

By the end of the phone call Trevor had promised to put a surveillance team on Brian, but what he didn't tell Susan was that the police budget did not run to paying for a team of surveillance cops, his was a small Provincial OPP branch, not on a city budget. Instead, he decided that he would go under-cover and keep an eye on Brian Henderson, it would get him out of the office and back on the streets where the action was and that was they way he liked it."

FORTY

The morning's guest speakers wrapped up and a buffet lunch was served, the conference would resume at 2:00 p.m. Brian took Tom to one side.

"I'll take you to the airport and you can catch the 2:30 p.m. plane back to London. I'm going to stay on."

Tom was so relieved although he had enjoyed the morning he knew that Rose would be anxiously waiting his return. After they had eaten their lunch Brian and Tom left the conference. Unbeknown to them, Trevor Manning watched them from his car as they left The Hilton Hotel and got into Brian's rented car. Keeping a good distance, he followed them.

Brian looked at his watch and then spoke to Tom.

"I thought that I'd make a little detour and drive you out to the Red-Deer Mine."

Tom looked at his watch and was clearly anxious not to miss his flight.

"Don't worry I'll get you to the airport on time."

Tom had a bad feeling about the so-called detour. He, like

Rose, did not trust Brian one single bit, something about his manner worried him and all his instincts cried out that Brian was up to no good. Tom pulled out his phone and sent Rose a short text message telling her that he would be catching the 2:30 flight to London, before putting his phone back in his pocket he pressed the RECORD button. If Brian was to try something, and hopefully he wouldn't, the recording could be used as incriminating evidence. Tom hoped and prayed that it would not come to that.

They drove in silence for a few kilometres and then Tom saw a large sign for The Red-Deer Mine. Brian turned right into the entrance, but instead of driving up to the main office, he swung left and drove to where Tom could see a rather iridescent and stagnant looking tailing-pond. Brian pulled the car over and stopped the engine. He opened the glove box and pulled out a small 45 Beretta. Turning to Tom he pointed the gun directly at him and said, "You know something, Tom, I've already committed one murder, so killing you should be easy. Oh, don't look so shocked; David had it coming to him, he owed so much money to those Ukrainians and when he failed to arrange for your accidental death, that's what did it for me. It was easy then to point the finger at the gang lords and torching their Audi I think was quite an inspired move on my part, don't you agree? Do you know what the hardest part of killing David was? It was trying to avoid getting his blood on my clothes, and boy, was he a bleeder. I managed to drag his body out of the back of the Lincoln and dump it in the pond with not a drop of blood on me. This time there will be no dragging of a body as you, my friend, are going to walk into the pond yourself and then when the water is up to your waist I will shoot you, all nice and clean. Then I'll drive the car to the airport and back to the conference and nobody will miss you until your lovely lady calls in the troops. Witnesses will say that they saw me drop you off at the airport and I'll get away with the perfect murder, again. Now get out of the car and don't for a minute think about running."

Tom got out of the car slowly and Brian quickly jumped out of the driver's seat and ran around to Tom's side. He felt a jab in his back and realized that Brian was poking him with the end of the pistol.

"Start walking and keep going until I tell you to stop."

For a minute Tom thought about submerging himself in the water and swimming underwater as far and as long as he could hold his breath. But then he looked at the toxic pond and realized that if he survived the assassin he would probably die of something far worse than a bullet wound. Suddenly, Tom felt an odd sense of detachment wash over him, it was like watching yourself from a distance almost as if it was a movie set. Out of the corner of his eye he suddenly noticed a movement a little way behind Brian. He turned his head and could clearly see a man, not any man, but Sergeant Manning.

Brian snarled at Tom, "Stop turning around and keep walking."

Trevor had parked his car at the entrance to the mine and had walked the rest of the distance on foot following the fresh tire tracks. From behind a slag heap he watched Tom get out of the parked car followed by Brian and then watched in horror as Brian jabbed his pistol into Tom's back. He moved in close enough to take a shot at Brian should he have to and in doing so he saw Tom turn his head. He knew that Tom was aware of his presence and hoped that would give him some comfort in what must be a terrifying time. He heard Brian shout at Tom to keep walking and it was then that Trevor took action.

Tom was up to his knees in sludgy water. The pond felt and smelt of decay and once more a sense of detachment seeped over him. He closed his eyes and willed an image of Rose before him, like a lovely dream. He waited for the shot to come, but instead he was jolted back to reality by the steely voice of authority. Sergeant Manning commanded Brian to lay down his weapon.

What happened next Tom will never fully know as he had his back to Brian when two gunshots pierced the air almost simultaneously. Tom turned and saw that both men were still standing and for a second he thought that no one had been shot and then, Brian's body crumpled slowly and fell to the ground. Sergeant Manning remained standing as Tom ran out of the water and bent down to where Brian lay dying. He could tell that the man was trying to say something, and so Tom bent over to try to hear what Brian was saying.

"Tell Sylvia that I love her." With a rattling gurgle Brian Henderson died.

Trevor walked over to Tom and helped him to his feet. Slapping him on his back he said, "I think that you've got a plane to catch."

TAILING PONDS

Environmental issues concerning tailing ponds include toxic and harmful chemicals such as ammonia, mercury, and naphthenic acids. The water containing these chemicals is toxic to animals, particularly aquatic organisms.

In some silver mines arsenic and lead is present in the fine dust found around the ponds. When it rains this fine dust is leached into the ground water causing major pollution.

Mine tailings are the materials left over after separating the product from the ore. The ponds can cause erosion and sinkholes. They often consist of fine particles suspended in water which have the potential to damage the environment by releasing toxic metals.

ABOUT THE AUTHOR

Over the past thirty years Judy has written twenty novellas, various collections of poetry and a number of plays. Judy wrote her first full length novel in 2013 and developed it into a series called the Rose Blair Murder Mysteries all set in the sleepy village of Bayfield on the beautiful shores of Lake Huron in Ontario, Canada.

Judy and her husband reside in Bayfield with their beloved dog Susie and cat Thomas and enjoy visits from their children and grandchildren.

After retiring Judy and her husband took on a new challenge in their lives. Purchasing land on the outskirts of Bayfield they have planted a six acre vineyard and are in the process of designing and building a boutique winery.

Life is beautiful and sweet. I feel so very blessed with all my wonderful family and friends who continually surround me with their love.

ALSO BY JUDY KEIGHTLEY

Murder at Bayfield Beach

Murder at the Croquet Club

Murder at Town Hall

Murder at the Marina

Murder at the Little Inn

Murder at the Retreat

Murder at Windmill Lake

Murder at Bayfield River

Murder at the Mine

FIND OUT MORE!

Find Cozy House Press online to read more great cozy mysteries!

www.cozyhousepress.com

COZY HOUSE PRESS
MAKE A DATE WITH MURDER

.

www.ingramcontent.com/pod-product-compliance
Lightning Source LLC
Chambersburg PA
CBHW020320260626
47156CB00004B/1303